DEAD RECKONING

DEAD RECKONING

Robert Furlani

Writers Club Press
San Jose New York Lincoln Shanghai

Dead Reckoning

Writers Club Press
an imprint of iUniverse, Inc.

For information address:
iUniverse, Inc.
5220 S. 16th St., Suite 200
Lincoln, NE 68512
www.iuniverse.com

ISBN: 0-595-21960-8

Printed in the United States of America

For my family

We will not tire, we will not falter, and we will not fail.

—George W. Bush

CHAPTER 1

Vietnam, 1968

Jimmy Taggert leaned his M–16 against a small tree, keeping it well within reach as he wiped the sweat from his brow with his bare arm. It was hot, hotter than hell. The cool, comforting breeze from the north had deserted his unit just after sunrise, a full twelve hours earlier. The air was heavy, so heavy it suffocated, never letting you get quite enough of it in your lungs, always leaving you thirsting for more. It was the middle of the dry season and hadn't rained in nearly a month, maybe longer. Everything was dry—bone dry. Only the deepest streams still flowed, most were little more than a rolling mat of scorched earth. Ants oozed through the deep crevices left in their wake. The cease–fire agreement, signed by the president, was two days short of a week old and was already on shaky ground. There were reports of North Vietnamese troop movement deep in the DMZ, just north of Hue.

Jimmy slid a *Camel* from the twisted pack he had tucked up behind the mesh on his helmet and struck a match against the butt of his pistol, never taking an eye off his M–16 or the Vietnamese landscape.

"Christ, it's fucking hot today, hotter than hell's kitchen," he complained, taking a couple of long, deliberate drags. His cracked, blistered lips curled around the cigarette. He pushed his bottom lip over just far enough to release the spent smoke, stroking his matted hair back with his hand at the same time. Jimmy stood a few inches over six feet and a dozen pounds over two hundred. His receding hairline no longer masked the diagonal scar that zigzagged across the upper–part of his forehead. He got the scar when he was ten. Walked into a rake that was hanging, facing in the wrong direction, in his father's tool shed.

"It's always fucking hot here," Bobby Ryan said, mooching a cigarette from Jimmy's helmet without bothering to ask. Bobby was a gabby redheaded kid who loved life in every way. There was never a dull moment with him around—he wouldn't allow it. He did zero to sixty in the blink of an eye. He was the kind of kid who never looked back—always heading somewhere at the speed of light.

Like Jimmy, he had his childhood scars too. He was missing his left earlobe, bit off by a raccoon when he was eight. Seems he was hell–bent on flushing it out from behind several cords of firewood. He managed to corner the critter fairly quickly, but was too young to know much about cornered animals, and before he could pull his freckled face back, the animal had a chunk of his ear. The truth of the matter is that the rabies shots hurt more than the bite. He found the wedge of his ear, shriveled and black, lying on the ground the next day. He saved it in a jar of formaldehyde and tried to bring it to show–and–tell until his teacher caught wind of it. Bobby settled for showing it to the *cooler* kids in his third grade class after school. He kept the ear for a week. He would have kept it longer but his mom found out where he stashed it and flushed it down the toilet like a dead goldfish from the county fair.

"Remember our first tour…remember how hot it was? Shit, I'd bet a six–pack and a squeeze of my girlfriend's big tits it was hotter that year. It was wetter, though; I'll give you that much. I bet I pissed more this week than it's rained in a month."

Jimmy laughed. "Is that a one handed squeeze or two you're offering? I'm sure Debbie would be glad to know you think so much of her tits." His lips curled into a narrow smile. "She's got a nice set though…that's for sure." He leaned forward and pushed his cigarette up against Bobby's until he could see a faint red glow.

Bobby nodded his appreciation and took a long drag, stoking the tip of his cigarette until there was a steadier glow. "Won't be long now before I get to climb on top of them myself. Hard to believe we'll be out of this fucking place in a few days, huh? What's the first thing you gonna do back home?"

"Ask Anne to marry me," Jimmy said without hesitation. "Can't wait to hold her again, smell her long blonde hair, kiss her like there ain't no tomorrow. Promise her I'll never leave again. And I won't. I've seen enough of the world. More than I figured I would…more than I wanted to. I'm figuring on picking up a ring in Saigon, before we bug out of here. I got close to six hundred saved; not counting the hundred–fifty Uncle Sam still owes me. Think that'll buy me a nice ring, one she'll be proud to show off to her friends?"

"Shit, that'll buy a big rock…a *fucking* big rock. The kind that gets you laid for a month. She'll have trouble holding up her hand. She'll need both arms to lift that sucker. Course, you know you're putting me in a jam. Don't you?"

"How's that?"

"Anne and Debbie have been friends for a long time…almost as long as us. Deb and me go further back than you and Anne, almost six months further. If you're showing up with a ring and all I'm hanging onto is a bunch of flowers when we step off the plane, then my ass is grass. Sure as shit it is, 'specially when Anne starts to wave that rock around like she's shooing away a swarm of bees near a jar of honey. Yeah, I won't get any that night. Maybe not for a lot of nights, not if all I'm holding is a wilted bunch of flowers." Bobby sucked hard on his cigarette, lifted his head, and blew a stream of smoke high into the hot air.

"I suppose I should ask too. Course, asking gets me in a whole other jam. I've got less than half of what you've stashed away. Didn't know my *best* friend was planning on getting hitched. Figured *he'd* tell me something like that sooner than *he did*...give me a chance to hustle up a little more scratch. Anne's rock's gonna be a whole lot bigger. Deb won't say nothing at first. She'll smile and hug me like nothing's wrong. Like nothing's bothering her. Not 'til we're alone anyway. Then I'll hear about how big Anne's ring is. She'll be asking why I couldn't buy her one as big. Shit, I won't get none that night either...maybe not for a week of nights, maybe longer, depending on how big a difference there is. I'm between a rock and a hard place, Jimmy. Damned if I do. Damned if I don't."

"Are you done jabbering? Christ, Bobby, if I didn't know you better I'd swear you got constipation of the brain and diarrhea of the mouth. Either that or the heat's got you all fouled up. We've been friends ever since my dad backed up the U–Haul in the driveway next to yours, halfway through third grade...haven't we? We've done everything together since then...right? Hell, we played on the same baseball and football teams for next to forever. If I wasn't handing the ball off to you, watching you pick up a hundred yards, I was hurling an eighty mile–per–hour slider your way on Abbott's Field. Man, we haven't missed spending two weeks wandering through old man Hadley's woods, hunting deer every November for the past ten years...have we?"

Jimmy loosened the laces on his boot and slid it off. He slowly pulled his sock off, exposing a badly swollen ankle, twice its normal size. It looked as if someone had filled it with a quart of water. The surrounding skin was a collage of deep purple and blue. He glanced at it for a brief moment, grimaced and massaged it with his hands as he continued. "What I'm saying to you is that we pool our money, split it down the middle, and buy two rings...same size. That is if you're serious about Deb. Don't do it just 'cause I'm doing it. Hell, we can still go hunting every November even if I'm married. We'll always be friends, man. Just like my mom says...like two peas in a pod."

Bobby smiled and held out his hand. "You got yourself a deal, partner. But I want to put in my fair share. I'll pay you back the difference just as soon as I cash my first paycheck back home. I won't shake on it 'til you agree. Uncle Joe's gonna get me a job at the mill, pouring steel. Pays close to five dollars an hour. Probably can get you in too if you want. Just say the word."

Jimmy shook his hand and smiled. "Deal. I'll pass on the mill for now. Figured I take the County Sheriff test in the fall. My dad said they give veterans ten points, sort of like extra credit I guess. I always wanted to wear a badge. Hang that piece of tin on my jacket, slide my sunglasses on and chase the hell out of kids bombing cars on Route 16, near the underpass, right where we used to toss 'em. Only I'll be a whole lot faster than Sheriff Heywood. A fat girl with one leg could outrun that slob."

Bobby nodded and laughed out loud. "Think we'll always be friends? Even when we're old and gray?"

"Yeah, I suppose so. You'll probably be hanging out at my house, drinking beer, bitching about your wife all night. I'll probably have to toss you out...tell you to go home to her," Jimmy snickered.

Bobby smiled. "Probably so. Christ, what happened to your foot? It looks pretty fucking bad."

"I twisted it really good a few days back. Hell, it's getting better. You should have seen it yesterday. I had a hell of a time getting my boot on."

"Hurt much?"

"Only when I walk," Jimmy grimaced, slipping his boot on and drawing the laces as tight as his ankle would allow.

"Time to move out," Captain O'Malley barked. "We've got to get back before dark. We're pulling back in the morning. Taggert!"

"Sir."

"Your turn for point. Go up a klick and a half, southeast of here. Stop at the pond and wait. I don't want too much jungle between you and us."

"Yes, Sir."

"Hey, Cap," Bobby said, walking up to O'Malley.

"Yeah, what is it, Ryan?"

"I'll take point for awhile."

Jimmy jumped in, "I got it covered, bro, thanks anyway."

"His ankle looks like a fat lady's leg, Cap. He ain't going to be much good up front. Not today anyway. Let me take his tour. He can pay me back when he's healed."

O'Malley turned to Taggert. "Fall back. Ryan's on point. Carson, you bring up the rear. Canfield, radio base, let 'em know we're headed in, should be there in an hour. Tell 'em to leave some chow for us. Let's go ladies, we ain't got all day."

"Roger that, Captain," Canfield replied, reaching for his walkie–talkie.

Jimmy tossed a cigarette to Bobby. "Thanks, man…I owe you."

"What are friends for? I'll catch you later."

Bobby slipped the cigarette in his pocket, put a fresh clip in his rifle, and headed south. Dusk wasn't far off. It would arrive sooner in the jungle. The thick foliage engulfed most of the sunlight. The mosquitoes were out in force, almost as thick as the air itself. He was already out of sight, a good distance ahead of the rest of the unit.

Jimmy tossed his spent cigarette on the ground, making sure he squeezed the fire out of it first. The ground was dry. It wouldn't take much to set it off, he knew.

Canfield and O'Malley were ahead of Jimmy; Carson, Wilson, and Masseti were a few yards back. They had all been together for a while, almost four months—everyone but Masseti. He was fresh out of boot camp. Signed up the day he turned eighteen, less than four months earlier. Jimmy and Bobby weren't a whole lot older. Jimmy turned twenty–one the same day Masseti turned eighteen and

Bobby, two months later. But there was a huge difference in their seasoning. Masseti was still cutting his teeth, just a young pup finding his way on the hunt.

Old–timers like Taggert and Ryan didn't like to be around new blood. Kids as green as Masseti can get you killed. It wasn't personal. They liked the kid, just didn't want to get shot because of him. Masseti knew it, understood it, but didn't like it. Being eighteen is hard enough. Being eighteen in 'Nam was next to impossible. He tried not to cry, at least not when anyone was looking. But there wasn't a day that went by that he didn't wish he was home, sitting on his porch, waiting for his girlfriend to stop by. He was the big man on campus in high school, captain of football and wresting, but that was good for shit in his present location. No one gave a rat's ass about that. Shooting a rifle was what mattered most. Killing the VC…that's what got you noticed. It's kill or be killed, that's the steady diet for the day.

Bobby had a strange feeling, like someone was watching him. He wasn't the type that was easily spooked. He hadn't seen or heard anything but had the feeling all the same. Trampling through the jungle is bad enough, but it's worse when it's dry. Everything makes noise. The twigs snap under your weight, sending off a series of sharp crunching noises that carry with the wind.

He was almost a klick ahead of his unit when he reached the pond. He stopped about ten yards from its edge, squatted down, and pulled a pair of binoculars from his backpack. It was a good–sized pond, 30 yards across at its widest part. Its banks were steep, and dropped down at least five feet. Most of the trees surrounding the water were set back a dozen feet or more. The distance between the tree line and water was thick with brush. Plants choked the fertile soil. They were green and fresh and contrasted sharply with the burnt foliage behind them. The water looked about four feet deep and inviting. It was probably twice that depth before the dry spell started. Its surface was taut. There wasn't a single ripple across its width. The water was clear, so clear that you could see schools of fish gliding through the weed–choked bottom.

"Christ, it's fucking hot," Bobby muttered. He scanned the pond, following its perimeter from one side to the other, looking for movement. *VC could be anywhere,* he thought. A sniper would have a field day. Sit in a tree, wait for a stray GI to waltz into view—maybe just hot and thirsty enough to let down his guard for a moment and steal a quick swim or drink. But Bobby had been around the block a couple of times and knew better. Masseti might just have been green enough to jump in the water without thinking, especially with it being so hot. Instead, he knelt down just inside the safety of the trees, camouflaged by their sprawling tarp and shadows cast by the setting sun.

His mind wandered for a moment, carrying him to a faraway place. It took him home to Darien—to the large pond on the southeast corner of old–man Hadley's farm where he and his best friend, Jimmy Taggert, used to spend the endless days of summer without a care in the world. It took him to a small farm that sat some 50 yards off a winding country road. He could see his father, sitting on the porch in his favorite chair, reading the evening paper with the radio on. A bottle of Genny Cream Ale rested on top of the railing, just within his father's reach. His black lab, Casey, was stretched out across the stairs. He saw his mother through the window, humming a song as she peeled potatoes at the kitchen sink. His brother and sister were setting the table, arguing over whose turn it was to wash the dishes. Lastly, he saw himself, walking down the long gravel driveway.

It was a driveway he hadn't set foot on since he joined the 82nd Airborne Division. His army–issued, olive green dufflebag was slung over his shoulder. A gentle breeze shuffled the sweet fragrance of his mother's cooking through the yard, along the whitewashed slatted fence. It lingered in the driveway, hovering over his head, begging him to come closer. Bobby shut his eyes for a moment and took it all in.

As he got closer, he could see the bright smile on his father's face just before he turned to yell to his mother. The wind picked up, gently bending the sprawling branches of a towering sycamore that sat on the edge of the driveway. A collection of oriental chimes that hung from the porch came to life. A moment later, the front door flew open and his mother rushed out to greet him. Her red and white checked apron was flapping in the cool summer breeze. Casey was already at his feet, jumping up and licking the stubble covering his face. There was a gleam in his father's eyes and overwhelming relief in his mother's. Their son was home—home for good.

Bobby never heard the light footsteps behind him until it was too late. A hand clamped onto his face, covering most of his nose and mouth. Another hand slid a knife up under his throat. The edge dug into his skin, stopping just short of cutting. He was yanked to his feet at the same time that his rifle was ripped from his grasp. Another hand snatched his revolver from its holster.

CHAPTER 2

"You move I kill," a voice said from behind him. A brief conversation, between his captors, followed. Bobby had been *in country* long enough to pick out some of the words—none of them were good.

"Turn round…slow. Fast I kill." His broken English was crude but effective.

Bobby turned as he was instructed, keeping his hands high in the air. His heart thumped wildly in his chest. The hairs on the back of his neck stood on end.

There were four VC. Three looked all of sixteen. None stood taller than five feet. Their eyes were dark and cold. All were skinny. It was the kind of skinny that makes you sick just looking at them, nothing but skin and bones. Dirt and grime coated their skin, making them appear darker than they were. Their body odor was offensive, their breath—worse. Their clothes were torn and tattered. Two didn't have shoes. One was missing four toes on one foot and three on the other. Three were just kids, orphaned by the war. The fourth was a VC regular, probably in his early twenties, the alpha dog of the pack. All of them had guns.

Bobby knew he was in worse shit than if he'd been surrounded by a dozen VC regulars with AK–47's loaded to the hilt. A pack of enraged teens on hormonal overload, whose parents were likely murdered in front of their eyes, is the worst kind of shit you can step into. They were looking for retribution. They were looking for blood.

He thought about running. He was fast, the fastest kid in his high school. He even held the state record in the 100–yard dash back in '65. The VC might be able to keep up with him for a hundred yards or so, but not too much more, not in their present condition. But he needed a diversion. He knew he wouldn't get two feet without one.

I have to stall. It's my only chance. The rest of the unit can't be more than ten minutes away by now, he thought.

Two Vietcong stood in front of him. Two stood several yards behind him. Each had a rifle trained at his head. The leader of the pack stepped forward, slid a rusty machete from its worn leather sheath, and held it under Bobby's sweaty throat. He stared for a moment, showing no emotion. His lifeless brown eyes never blinked. A smug smile slowly came to his face. His lips parted, exposing the few teeth he had. They were yellow and brown pegs, sunk into bloody, blackened gums. He spat a stream of brownish fluid at the ground near Ryan's feet.

"You lone?" the freakish looking VC asked, wiping his mouth with his filthy sleeve.

"Yeah," Bobby replied, swallowing hard.

The edge of the machete dug into his throat a little harder.

"Where friends?"

"I don't know, I got separated from them a day ago. I'm lost."

"You lie."

Bobby could feel the others move in closer behind him. The way pack animals do when they're ready to pounce, when the air is thick with the smell of the kill. He was out of time and he knew it.

This time the machete drew blood.

* * *

"Anybody know what's on the menu tonight?" Canfield asked.

"What does it matter? It all tastes the same," Taggert replied.

Captain O'Malley threw his two cents worth in, "I don't give a rat's ass what it is. I'm starving."

"Probably rice served on top of rice. Fucking gook food again," Canfield whined. "I've been eating so much rice that I'm gonna start looking like a gook. My mom probably won't recognize me when I go home."

"We'll be coming up on the pond soon. It's just over that—"

Canfield's walkie–talkie barked. "Who the fuck there?" The VC's voice echoed through the thick evening air.

Captain O'Malley spun sharply, raised one hand in the air and signaled for the unit to stop.

Canfield lowered the volume and handed the set to the captain as the rest of the men took defensive positions south of the ridge. Taggert checked to make sure the clip on his rifle was engaged as he squatted down next to the captain. His eyes darted everywhere, scanning the landscape. Masseti and Wilson took the flanks. Carson slid down an embankment behind them and Canfield took point.

"Hello, American mudder–fuckers. We got you boy. We gonna kill you boy. You listen good. We kill you soon. Real soon."

Taggert reached for the walkie–talkie but O'Malley pulled it away before he could get a hand on it.

"No, Taggert. That's what they want."

"Maybe the slope's lying. Maybe they found Ryan's walkie–talkie—that's all. Maybe he got away. Maybe it's a fucking trick," Wilson said.

An excruciatingly long moment of silence followed. Canfield squatted, bracing his back against a tree. "What the fuck's going on?" he asked.

The first scream was the longest and the worst. The VC had more than Bobby's walkie–talkie.

"FUCK YOU, GOOK!" Bobby yelled.

You could hear the knife being plunged into his chest. Another scream, duller than the first, was followed by a gurgling sound, then by moans.

"FUCK YOU, GI JOE," the VC shouted. The gratification in his tone hung in the air. The other VC's were laughing, almost howling.

Taggert jumped up and rushed toward the pond. O'Malley's outstretched arm fell just inches short of his leg.

"TAGGERT…STOP!" O'Malley yelled. His voice fell on deaf ears. Taggert had already passed Canfield and was accelerating. He never gave his battered ankle a second thought as he pushed through the dense brush.

"Son–of–a–fucking–bitch!" The captain grunted as he rose to his feet. "Give Taggert back up. COME ON. LET'S MOVE IT."

Bobby was still alive, barely, when Jimmy reached him. He was lying on his side, curled up in the fetal position. A pool of blood collected alongside his body. A narrow stream had formed in the dirt and was rolling down the bank toward the water. His feet were bare. His backpack and rifle were gone. Jimmy eased him to his back. The front of his shirt was soaked in blood, so much blood that you could wring it out. Bobby's left ear was gone, cut from his head. A bloody, jagged stump was all that remained. The rest of the unit arrived and took up defensive positions along the perimeter. Jimmy pressed against the wounds littering Bobby's chest with his bare hands, trying desperately to quell the bleeding.

"GET A FUCKING MEDEVAC CHOPPER IN HERE. NOW!" Jimmy screamed, still pressing on the holes in his friend's chest. "TELL THEM TO BRING BLOOD…LOTS OF BLOOD."

"I'm here, Bobby. I'm here now. You're going to be okay. They're getting a bird for you. It'll be here any second now. Hang in there, man. Hang in there, damn it!"

Bobby struggled to speak. Blood was collecting in his lungs, leaving little room for air. He was wheezing badly, almost gagging. "Hottest day of the year and I'm cold, Jimmy. I'm fucking cold. That can't be good," he said faintly. "You're my best friend. Best friend I ever had. Glad I took point. Glad it wasn't you."

"Don't speak, Bobby. Save your strength. I got a blanket in my backpack. It'll keep you warm. I'll go get it. I'll be right—"

"No! Don't leave me," Bobby pleaded, grabbing hold of Jimmy's sleeve. His grip was weak, almost nonexistent. "I don't want to die alone."

The wheezing became more pronounced and he began coughing up blood—dark red blood, almost purple. Jimmy had never seen blood that dark before. "CHRIST, WHERE'S THAT FUCKING CHOPPER?" he yelled again. Blood surged from Bobby's chest with each cough, spilling onto his fatigues. Gravity pulled the narrow stream of blood closer to the water. Vultures circled overhead, patiently waiting for their turn at the table.

"You're not gonna die, Bobby. No way. You're not going die…not today…not in 'Nam."

Bobby was losing consciousness. His chest was heaving. His pulse was weak. "Jimmy?" he said. His voice was faint, barely audible. His lips were losing their color. A bluish tint formed at their edge.

"Yeah, Bobby, I'm right here, man. Right next to you."

"Promise me you'll tell my mom and dad that I love 'em. Will ya?"

"You're gonna tell them yourself. You ain't gonna die, Bobby. You're too damn stubborn. You're not going to die…I won't let you!"

"Promise me, Jimmy. Swear to it."

Jimmy took his hand, held it tight and nodded. "I promise, but you're going to—"

A faint smile made it to Bobby's face just before he took his last breath. His chest heaved one last time as the air left his lungs forever.

"NO! GODDAMN IT…NO!" Jimmy cried. He bent forward, covered his friend's body, and sobbed.

Captain O'Malley knelt down next to Jimmy and put his hand on his shoulder. Neither man spoke for a long while.

The Huey broke over the ridge and hovered overhead. It landed in a small clearing on the south side of the pond.

"We've got to load him in the chopper now, Jimmy. We've got to get out of here. The sun will be down in a half–hour, maybe less," Captain O'Malley said quietly.

Jimmy wiped away the tears with his bloody hand and nodded slightly.

O'Malley motioned for Masseti and Wilson to load Bobby's body onto the chopper.

Jimmy shook his head and stepped between them. "I'll do it," he said, bending forward and hoisting the body up.

Masseti and Wilson stepped aside and let him pass.

Jimmy was halfway to the Huey and out of earshot when Masseti spoke up.

"Why did they cut off his ear?" he asked.

Wilson drew a pinch of chewing tobacco from a can of *Skoal* and tucked it into the corner of his mouth, between his cheek and gum. He offered Masseti a pinch before sliding the can back into his pocket. "VC cut 'em off, thread a string through 'em and make a necklace out of 'em…wear it like some fucking badge of honor…show it off to their gook friends, fucking bastards. They're goddamn animals…every last one of 'em."

"I shot this gook last tour. It was a good shot…he must have been a hundred yards away, maybe more. Anyway, when I got to him he was crawling. Like they make us do in boot. You know, pulling yourself with your arms, dragging your feet. A round must of tore into his spine. He was trying to get to the jungle cause all his gook buddies were dead. Stupid son–of–a–bitch even forgot his rifle. I watched him crawl for a minute, let him get close to the trees. He looked like a 'gator heading for the swamp…only slower," Wilson said, spitting a mouth full of saliva and tobacco on the ground. "He couldn't have been more than a couple of yards from the trees when I walked up to him and rolled him over. The gook bastard was wearing a necklace...had fourteen ears on it...FOURTEEN FUCKING EARS. And you know what the gook says to me?"

"What?"

"Don't shoot."

Masseti raised an eyebrow. "That fucker asked you not to shoot him?"

"Don't shoot. Can you fucking believe it? *Don't shoot.*"

"What did you do?"

"I had a good chew going, just like I do now. I stood over him and spit in his fucking face. He was too scared to move, didn't even raise a hand to wipe if off his face. I watched it slide down his forehead into those slanted little eyes of his. Looked like it burned some 'cause he squinted and his eyes watered a bunch. I reached down, tore the necklace off, shoved it in his mouth, and made him eat it. Then I popped him, four to the head, ten to the body. One for each ear. Only good gook's a dead gook, if you ask me."

Masseti had a sinking feeling in the pit of his stomach.

"Hey, Captain. There are four sets of footprints over there, heading north. Should we follow them?" Canfield asked.

"No. It's too late. We're just about out of sun. Climb into the egg–beater."

"Yes, Sir."

O'Malley turned toward the chopper. "Okay, everyone in. We're getting out of here. Let's go. Move it."

Canfield, Wilson, Masseti, and Carson had already climbed aboard when Taggert approached O'Malley.

"You know I can't get on that bird, Captain. I'd be the one in the body bag if it weren't for Bobby taking point. I've got unfinished business out here. There's a reckoning that needs to happen. I can't go home and face his folks. Not 'til I make things right. They killed him for sport...even laughed about it. That ain't no way for a soldier to die. We go too far back for me to climb on that chopper and put this behind me. You can order me to get on her but I won't. So let me do what I have to. Let me do it for Bobby."

O'Malley looked at him, looked deep into his eyes. He could see that the life had left them. There was nothing there. Everything had been pushed away by hate, the kind of hate that consumes someone. "We're bugging out at 1200 hours...not a second later. We'll leave without you if you're not back."

Jimmy nodded and turned toward the trees.

"Jimmy," Captain O'Malley yelled over the loud hum of the Huey.

Taggert looked over his shoulder.

"I'm sorry about Bobby. He was a hell of a soldier."

"He was a hell of a friend." Jimmy turned and disappeared into the darkness of the jungle.

The chopper climbed above the trees a few seconds later. Its silhouette hung on the setting sun before disappearing behind a mountain range. The hum of its engine lingered for a while longer before slowly fading away. Jimmy followed the VC's trail for about forty–five minutes until their footprints were buried by the darkness. A full moon, partially eclipsed by the clouds, cast eerie shadows across the lowlands. A light breeze picked up, gently stroking the long blades of elephant grass that skirted the tree line. He sat down, slid his back against a large tree, and rested. He'd have to wait until daybreak to track them again. He knew they wouldn't travel at night, not with a full moon.

His mind was still fresh with the haunting image of Bobby's bloody body strewn along the edge of the water. It was forever burned into his memory. He could hear the Vietcong's laughter echoing through the jungle as they plunged the machete deep into his best friend's chest. He closed his eyes, trying instead to remember Bobby in happier times, but the images were too raw, too real, and too painful to let go so easily. The evening passed slowly. The jungle was full of life. Crickets kept a steady beat and owls called out into the darkness. A solitary bullfrog croaked from some faraway pond, hoping for a reply that never came. A thousand different noises flooded the darkness. Their constant hum lent comfort to the tired soldier. He knew he was safe as long as the noise continued. It's when the jungle is silent that you have to worry, when animals pick up the scent of man. The better part of an hour passed before he drifted off to sleep. It would be his last night in Vietnam.

CHAPTER 3

Jimmy was on his feet at first light. The gentle breeze that came with the night was pushed away by the morning sun as it began to heat the air. He followed the Vietcong's trail as it twisted through the thick brush. The jungle grew silent as he approached the top of a small ravine, less than two klicks from the pond. He dropped to his knees, then to his stomach, and crawled toward its rugged crest.

He could hear voices, Vietnamese voices, floating in the air. He peered out over the edge and saw the four Vietcong. Two were sitting beside a tree, the other two were standing, looking at a map. The VC regular had Bobby's M–16 draped over his shoulder and Bobby's pistol tucked into his pants, alongside his walkie–talkie. They were standing in the middle of a ravine that ran for about one hundred fifty yards.

Jimmy slid back down the ridge and crept along its edge, staying low to the ground. He followed the ravine until it spilled out into a narrow clearing, no larger than half of a city block. He swung his backpack down off his shoulder and grabbed four Claymore mines, stacking them in a pile on the ground. He reached into another pocket and pulled out a length of trip wire. He buried the mines at the edge of the clearing in a semicircular pattern, spacing them fifteen feet apart. He connected all four with trip wire, hiding it in the tall grass.

Jimmy doubled back until he was fifty yards south of their camp and quietly worked his way back toward the Vietcong. He squatted down behind a large tree just fifteen yards from where they stood. Three were gathered around the map now, arguing over which way to go. The other was heading toward him. Jimmy rested his rifle against the tree, and slid his knife from its sheath and his pistol from its holster.

The VC stopped in front of a row of small trees, less than five yards from where Jimmy lay waiting. He stepped forward, deeper into the privacy of the trees, and slid his pants down to his ankles. He began to squat until he felt a hand cover his mouth and the sharp edge of a knife against his throat.

"Those boots you're wearing belonged to my friend. He's the one you butchered by the pond yesterday," Jimmy said in a steely whisper.

He thrust the knife deep into the VC's throat and pulled harshly. Its sharp blade easily tore through the flesh and cartilage, opening the throat from one end to the other. A stream of blood poured out, splattering the trees and littering the dirt. The VC's eyes bulged and his body heaved as the air left his lungs for good. Jimmy glanced over his shoulder as he eased the body to the ground. He bent forward, took Bobby's boots off the VC's feet, tied the laces together, and slung them over his shoulder.

A huge cloud drifted across the blue sky, blocking the bright sun and casting a shadow across the ravine. The other Vietcong were preparing to break camp. Two were standing side by side, smoking the morning's first cigarette. The VC regular was a few yards to their left, gathering the supplies. Jimmy's first shot thundered through the jungle, easily finding its mark, exploding half of the VC's skull on impact. Fragments of brain and bone pelted the trees. The soldier's detached jaw fell to the ground; a cigarette still wedged between his yellow teeth. The second VC didn't have time to raise his rifle before five rounds tore through his body, lifting him off the ground. His lifeless body crumpled to the dirt, landing on top of his friend. Blood quickly colored the jungle floor. Jimmy pivoted sharply, trained his sights on the VC regular, and emptied his clip. The VC took off, running through the ravine, using the trees for cover. Jimmy pursued him, sliding in another clip as he raced through the dense brush. The sun slipped under the cloud. Its bright light flooded the forest again. The VC kept running, blindly firing his rifle behind him. Jimmy kept coming, peppering the landscape with round after round.

An explosion abruptly ended the chase a split second after the VC hit the clearing. He was lying on his back, a few yards into the clearing when Jimmy caught up with him. Both legs were gone, one at the knee, the other at the hip. Small pieces of flesh and bone, all that remained of his lower limbs, were scattered throughout the clearing. Huge blackbirds swooped down from the tall trees, snatching the most distant pieces of flesh. Jimmy yanked Bobby's pistol from the VC's belt and stood over his mangled body. He stared for a long moment before reaching down and tearing the necklace with Bobby's ear on it from the soldier's skinny neck.

Jimmy pulled the VC's machete from its sheath and thrust it deep into the bloody stump. "Hurts…doesn't it, motherfucker?" he grunted, gritting his teeth. "Fuck you and your goddamn country you toothless bastard."

The VC's scream echoed through the treetops, momentarily scaring the birds from their meal.

"His name was Bobby Ryan."

Jimmy pushed the barrel of Bobby's pistol up to the VC's forehead and cocked the hammer.

"He was my best friend."

He squeezed the trigger until the clip was empty.

Masseti tapped Canfield on the shoulder and pointed to the tree line. Jimmy Taggert emerged from the jungle. He waded through the tall blades of grass and brush that eventually gave way to the cut grass surrounding the camp

"Hey, Cap. He's back! Taggert's back," Masseti yelled from across the compound.

Captain O'Malley stepped out of his tent as Jimmy reached the camp. "Did you set things right?" he asked.

Jimmy nodded.

"Good. I knew you would. I talked with HQ this morning. I've got you on a chopper heading home. It leaves in an hour. Ryan's on it too...thought you'd want to bring him home to his folks."

"Thanks, Captain. I've got to find the doc...see if he can sew Bobby's ear back on. I don't want his folks seeing him without it. Losing a son is bad enough. They don't need to see that too."

O'Malley gave a slight nod. "Forget about this place, Jimmy. Don't bring the war back to Darien. Leave it here where it belongs. Leave it in this god–forsaken place."

Jimmy climbed aboard the Huey and tossed his dufflebag in the back, next to the row of body bags that filled its belly. He looked out the bay door as the chopper rose above the camp, still clutching his M–16 with both hands. The camp quickly disappeared from sight, replaced by green Vietnamese countryside. He leaned back, rested his head against the warm steel, closed his eyes, and thought about his best friend. He could still picture Bobby with his toothy smile and freckled face. He could still hear the sound of his raspy laugh. Tears ran down his face, dripping onto his fatigues as the chopper turned south toward Saigon.

CHAPTER 4

Darien, 1998

It was a typically quiet Saturday morning in Darien. Fall had arrived much earlier than most years. The jet stream had dipped sharply south, bringing with it a blast of frigid air from Canada. A thick morning fog covered the lowlands. A steady wind tugged the few remaining leaves from the trees, scattering them across village streets. Wood burning stoves and fireplaces filled the air with their unmistakable scent. A brown squirrel, with acorns stuffed in its baggy cheeks, dodged early morning traffic en route to its lofty nest.

Jimmy Taggert walked hand–in–hand with his wife along Main Street. The wind was at their backs and the sun was in their eyes.

"Hey, Sheriff, just a couple of weeks left now, huh?" Billy Stoner yelled from across the street. He had a newspaper in one hand and a cup of coffee in the other. A steady flow of steam rose from the small hole in its lid.

"Yep, twelve days to go," Jimmy said with a wave.

"I saw that RV thing of yours parked at Danny's garage the other day. He must have been giving her a tune–up or something. It sure is a big one. I don't know that I've ever seen one that big before. Bet it set you and the misses back quite a few, huh?"

"Yep, quite a few, Billy."

Stoner smiled. "I thought so. Shotgun season starts in a few weeks. Where you headed this year? Same place as usual?"

"Nope. I'm going to sit this one out. Figured I got my share of deer over the years."

Billy nodded slowly. "I suppose so," he muttered.

"Have a good day, and say hello to your mom for me. Tell her I'm planning on swinging by her place later in the week. Tell her I'm likely to have time for a slice of her homemade apple pie...maybe even time for two," Jimmy said, with a wink and a smile.

"I'll tell her. I dropped off two and half bushels of apples last week. She ain't stopped baking since. Old man Riley says the smell's driving him half–crazy. Told me he's gonna steal one if she puts it on the sill again."

"I couldn't arrest him for doing that...not with the way her pies taste," Jimmy said, shaking his head and laughing. "That's too much temptation for any man."

He walked his wife to the front of the First National Bank and kissed her goodbye. "I'll swing by and pick you up at one o'clock. What do you say we grab a bit of lunch afterwards?"

Anne Taggert smiled. "Are you buying?" she joked.

Jimmy laughed. "I was hoping you'd bring home a few samples from the vault."

"Well, I could, but then you'd have to arrest me, seeing that you're the sheriff and all."

"Hmm, that might not be a bad idea. I'd have to cuff you...take you back to the house for questioning."

Anne laughed. "Oh, I'm sure you'd like that."

"You got that right! I don't think I'd get any complaints from you either."

"No, I don't suppose you would."

"Don't give all the money away. I'll see you in four hours."

"Don't be late," Anne said.

"I'll be here...one o'clock sharp. I promise."

"What'll it be, Sheriff?"

"I've been coming here every Saturday for close to thirty years. Haven't I, Sam?"

"Yep, thirty years sounds about right."

"And I get the same haircut each and every time. Don't I?"

"Yep. Thin out the sides…trim the top a bit."

Jimmy scratched his head. "Then can you explain to me why you ask me how I want my hair cut *every* time I climb into this chair of yours?"

"Ain't no explanation needed, Sheriff. It's just the way it is. I still have to ask. Supposing you decided you wanted something different and I started clipping away before you had a chance to speak up. Then it'd be too late. I couldn't fix it 'til next time you came in. If you wanted something real different then a month might have to pass before I could cut it right. I can't assume nothing. Not in this business anyhow. Besides, you know what they say about assuming something. Don't you?"

"Yep, you make an ass out of you and me."

"That's right."

Jimmy shook his head and laughed out loud. "Thin out the sides and take a little off the top. Okay?"

"Just like always, huh?" Sam said grinning.

"Yeah, just like always, Sam."

Jimmy sat in the barber chair gazing out the large plate glass window overlooking Main Street. He could see two blocks in either direction, from the Darien Coffee Shop to Wilson's Five and Dime store. First National Bank, a stone's throw from the corner, was the largest building on either block. Jimmy watched his wife slide the deadbolt over and open the bank for the day's business. A group of Saturday morning regulars had already formed a makeshift line at the door. They quickly funneled into the bank, passbooks in hand.

"So, you and Mrs. T are going to travel the country in that big house on wheels you just bought, huh?"

"Yep, we've got four kids and a litter of grandchildren scattered across this country and we're planning on visiting each of 'em for a spell…maybe longer."

"You sure you want to retire? Hell, you're just a shade over fifty."

"I've been the Sheriff for close to twenty years and Deputy Sheriff for ten before that. The kids are grown and on their own, and the house is bought and paid for. Anne and I want to travel while we're still young enough to enjoy it. We've been able to stash away a bit over the years. It ain't much but we don't need a whole lot either. It's time, Sam. Richie's a good man. He'll make a good Sheriff. It'll be good for Darien to get some young blood in here for a change."

"Maybe so, but you still seem too young to me," Sam mused. "Yep, too damn young, if you ask me."

Jimmy spread the newspaper across his lap and started to skim it as Sam meticulously cut his hair.

The door swung open, and an elderly woman stepped into the barbershop, bringing the cold autumn air with her. She was wearing a long wool coat. A white scarf with red stripes was neatly tucked under the burly coat. A small gold flag was pinned to her lapel. Its red, white and blue had faded away years earlier. Her gait was slow and deliberate. Her steps were short but steady.

Sam put his scissors down and took a few steps toward her.

She held out her hand and shook her head. "Get back to your cutting, Sam. I put the coat on by myself and I'm perfectly capable of taking it off by myself," she said, in a voice that defied the frailty of her body.

Jimmy smiled.

"It sure is a cold one this morning, boys."

"Yes, Mrs. Ryan, it sure is," Jimmy agreed.

"Your wife helped me with my weekly banking this morning. She said I'd find you over here. I swear, that woman hasn't aged a bit over the years. I don't know how she stays so young. You're looking a bit long in the tooth, Jimmy. But not her, Anne looks as pretty as the day you two got married. You'd best keep an eye on her. She's apt to find a young buck if you don't."

Jimmy laughed. "Thanks for the compliment…*I think!* What brings you here today?"

Mrs. Ryan cleared the magazines from a chair and sat down. "Veterans Day is a week from Wednesday. We're having a service for Bobby…ten o'clock at the church. It's been thirty years since he passed on and I was hoping you could say a few words. It won't be too long. Father's got a baptism at eleven."

The smile left Jimmy's face. "I'll be there, Mrs. Ryan. I'd be honored to say a few words. Thirty years…it's hard to believe it's been that long," he said quietly.

Mrs. Ryan swallowed hard and forced a smile. "Good. Can you come over for lunch afterwards? I'd appreciate the company."

Jimmy nodded and smiled. "I'd like that. I'd like that a lot. I'll bring the dessert."

"Just as long as your wife makes it. I'm not eating anything you've whipped together. I've seen you in the kitchen and it isn't pretty."

"You've got a point there, Mrs. R. I'll ask Anne to make a batch of cookies or something. You'll be safe from food poisoning that way. How's that—"

Jimmy's walkie–talkie came to life. The dispatcher's voice cut into the conversation.

"We've got a report of a car–deer accident up on Route 7, a mile and a half north of the Jacob farm. Can you get that, Richie?"

"Roger that, Max. ETA is 40 minutes."

Sam shook his head. "It's getting to be that time of the year. Bucks will be in full rut soon. They'll be going crazy…crazier than shit–house rats. I hope no one was hurt," he added.

Jimmy tossed the newspaper down and adjusted the volume on the walkie–talkie. "It's still a bit early in the season…a few weeks early," he noted.

The door swung open again and Johnny McCoy rushed inside, half out of breath. The sleeves of his blue and red flannel shirt were rolled up to his elbows, exposing a soiled white thermal undershirt. An enormous beer belly hung over his belt, completely eclipsing its silver buckle. Shoots of blonde hair jutted out from underneath a faded Cleveland Indian's baseball cap and the legs of his favorite pair of jeans were stuffed into a pair of steel–toed work boots. "What's goin' on with the Hatfield twins? Did you arrest the little bastards yet? I'll shoot 'em next time they set a foot on my property. Sure as I'm standing here…I'll pepper their rear ends with a load of buck-shot. They won't be able to sit for a month…maybe longer." There was a certain sense of satisfaction in his voice.

"Cool your jets, Johnny, and get a grip. You're not gonna shoot anyone. I talked with the Hatfields yesterday. Sat down with their folks and explained how they tore up your field doing doughnuts with their four wheeler. Hank wasn't too happy to say the least. I'm guessing he whipped their bottoms just as soon as my squad car cleared the driveway. Anyhow, I'm not gonna arrest them. I've decided—"

"What you mean, you're not gonna arrest them! They did five hundred dollars of damage to my field," Johnny interrupted. His face was as red as his shirt. The veins on his forehead bulged.

Jimmy swiveled the chair until he was facing Johnny. He reached into his top pocket, pulled out a toothpick, and slid it into the corner of his mouth. "Fifteen years ago I came across a group of high school kids trashing mailboxes with M–80s. Did most of the damage along Route 16 where the creek winds along the road for a spell…not too far from your dad's place. They were all liquored up, as I recall. A lot of folks wanted me to lock 'em up and throw away the key. I didn't see the need to arrest any of 'em, though. An arrest record tends to follow people quite a long time. It can really mess someone up later in life. Can't see doing that, 'specially when they'd been drinking and all. Nope, I didn't arrest any of 'em. I made 'em fix the mailboxes and cut the folk's lawn for the rest of the summer, though. They learned their lesson…each and everyone one." He looked up and winked. "You cut quite a few lawns that summer. Didn't you?"

Johnny turned his head and stared out the window. "Uh, yeah…I suppose I did, Sheriff," he grumbled.

"Yep, I suppose you did. I told the Hatfield twins to stop by your house the day after tomorrow. I told 'em you'd have a list of things that need fixin' and doin'. I figured they'd work on weekends 'til they've crossed everything off that list of yours. How's that sound?"

Johnny forced a smile. "It sounds just about right to me, Sheriff. I'll have a good long list for 'em."

"I expect you will."

Johnny turned and left as quickly as he came. The sound of Sam and Mrs. Ryan's laughter followed him out the door.

"That boy's going to give himself a good case of hemorrhoids, at the rate he's going," Nattie Ryan joked.

"He'd better include picking up a box of *Preparation H* on that list he's writing for the Hatfield twins," Sam said, and laughed.

Mrs. Ryan stood and put her coat on. "Well, boys, I best be getting back before my husband wakes up and realizes I'm not home. I'll see you at the service, Jimmy."

"I'll be there. Ten o'clock sharp."

"It wouldn't hurt you none to see the inside of a church for a change, Sam Barton," she said, reaching for the door.

"Yes, ma'am."

"Good. Don't be late and make sure you're wearing a tie."

Sam nodded sheepishly just before she turned and walked out the door. He couldn't see the broad grin that covered most of her face.

"She's one tough lady. Ain't she?" Jimmy said.

"I might use a more colorful adjective but—"

Jimmy's walkie–talkie lit up again.

"Got another report of a car–deer accident. This one's in the southtowns, a quarter mile from the county line on Route 20A. Richie's all the way at the other corner of the county. Can you get this one, Steve?"

"Yep, I'm on it, Maximus. Tell them I'll be there in twenty…fifteen if I don't get stuck behind any white–tops out for a Saturday drive in the country."

Sam scratched the only patch of hair left on his head. "Wonder what's spooking the deer this morning?" he asked.

"You better finish my cut, Sam. I'm the only car left in the town. I'll have to respond to the next call."

"I'll have you out of here in no time, Sheriff. I just got to trim the sides a bit and shave your neck."

An old black Cadillac pulled up on a side street adjacent to the First National Bank and parked. It was the same black Cadillac that had crept by the bank fifteen minutes earlier. Jimmy watched as three men, wearing long coats, climbed out and slowly walked into the bank. The driver stayed behind the wheel, calmly smoking a cigarette.

Jimmy slid his walkie–talkie out from under the gray apron and pressed the talk button. "Max, it's Jimmy."

"Yeah, boss, I'm here…go ahead." Max answered a moment later.

"Who called in the car–deer accidents? You got a name on either one?"

"Nope, both were anonymous. Neither caller wanted to leave his name. Why? Something wrong?"

"When's the last time you got a report of a car–deer accident where the caller didn't leave his name?" Jimmy asked.

"I can't recall…maybe never. What's going on?"

"Two reports of car–deer accidents, minutes apart, on opposite ends of the county. Neither caller leaves a name. I don't like it, Max.

Get Richie and Steve on the radio. Tell 'em to turn around and meet me at the bank. Tell 'em to kill the siren and lights when they get close to town. A black Caddy, carrying four men, just pulled up at the bank. Something ain't right. I got a bad feeling 'bout this."

"I'll meet you there in the blink of an eye," Max said anxiously. There was a noticeable quiver in his voice.

"No, stay put. I need you there. Tell Richie and Steve to hurry. Tell them Anne's working today."

"Roger that, Sheriff. I'll have them turned around faster than you can shake a stick."

"Good deal, Max. I'm going silent for a while. I'll contact you when I can." Jimmy turned his walkie–talkie off, stood up, and pulled the apron from his neck, letting it fall onto the small piles of hair covering the floor. "I need to borrow your jacket, Sam."

"It's yours. You need anything else?"

"Yeah, give me the pistol you have stashed under the cash register. The one I'm not suppose to know about."

Sam stepped over to the cash register and retrieved a 38–caliber pistol from a small drawer. "Here you go," he said as he handed the pistol over. "Be careful, it's loaded."

Jimmy took the pistol, stashed it in his boot, and rushed out the door as he slipped Sam's coat on, pulling the zipper up high enough to cover his badge. The cold air bit into his skin, sending a chill through his body. He crossed the street, being careful not to draw suspicion to himself.

Main Street was busier than usual. Cars lined both sides of the street for three–and–a–half blocks. A group of teenagers was hanging out in front of the music store. Each had a cigarette stuffed in a corner of their mouth. The boys were taking turns showing off their skateboarding prowess to girls who pretended to be impressed. A crew of town workers, dressed in orange, was huddled around a cherry picker. Each was slugging back a cup of steaming hot coffee as one of their colleagues struggled to change a bulb on a streetlight.

Jimmy stopped in front of the teenagers for a moment, keeping an eye on the car and bank.

"Yo, Sheriff! What's up?" Mark Coleman asked as he deftly flipped the blue skateboard up and snatched it from the air without looking.

"Give me a cigarette and move around the corner. Don't run…walk. I don't have time to explain. Just do it," Jimmy said quietly, but sternly. Narrow eyes conveyed the seriousness of his request.

Coleman's fingers fumbled in his coat pocket as he reached for his *Camels*. "Here you go, Sh—Sheriff," he stammered.

Jimmy's lips closed around a cigarette for the first time in twenty years and an old habit, which was once familiar and comforting, seemed foreign and unappealing. He slipped his service revolver into the coat pocket, slid the safety off, and approached the black Caddy from the rear.

The driver was a dark haired man from New Orleans by the name of Billy Joe Bouchard. A ragged beard covered much of his face. Bright sunlight reflected off his black, wire–rimmed sunglasses. The collar on his black leather jacket was pulled up, covering most of his neck. Billy's hair was cut short; a black baseball cap hid all but the back. Three large black letters, WCW, were embroidered on a white oval patch that was stitched to the front of the cap. A cigarette, half–spent, dangled from his thin lips. The four windows were rolled all the way down and the engine was running. Tufts of white smoke billowed from the exhaust.

Jimmy walked along the sidewalk until he was parallel with the Caddy's front window. He stopped, patted his coat, and checked his pockets, pretending to look for matches. Billy nervously glanced in his direction, taking his eyes off the bank's front doors for just a split–second or two.

"Hey buddy, ya got a light?" Jimmy asked as he bent forward and leaned into the window, resting his elbows on the door. "I can't find my lighter…must be in the pocket of my other coat, or maybe the kids took it again. Damn kids, they're always messing with my shit."

Jimmy pretended not to notice the sawed–off shotgun, partially covered by the morning paper, lying on the backseat.

Bouchard stared for a moment, let out an audible sigh, and reluctantly reached into his pocket. Sunlight caught the butt of the chrome–handled, 9mm pistol he had tucked under his leather jacket. "Here, keep the pack," he said reaching across the front seat.

The coat Jimmy was wearing hung down as he leaned forward and stretched for the matches, exposing most of his silver badge. Its shiny reflection lit up the driver's sunglasses. Billy Joe jerked his hand back, letting the matches fall to the seat, and reached for his gun.

Jimmy drew his a split–second sooner. "Ease your hand away from the gun and put both hands on the wheel," he said abruptly.

Bouchard didn't respond right away. He kept his hand near the pistol while weighing his options.

Jimmy cocked the hammer on his revolver. "I'm not asking again."

Billy reluctantly pulled his arm away and placed it on the steering wheel.

"Take your left hand and grab the butt of your pistol with two fingers. Ease it out of the holster and toss it over here. Keep your right hand on the steering wheel. Do it nice and slow."

"You don't have any idea who you're fucking with. Do you, Sheriff?"

"Do I look like I give a rat's ass?" Now quit stalling and give me the gun." Jimmy's eyes were narrow and cold, his voice, steady and strong.

The driver slowly slid his gun from its holster and placed it on the front seat. Jimmy collected the pistol, shoved it into his pocket, and opened the car door. "Now turn the engine off and throw me the keys. You know the drill. Use your left hand just like before."

"You're not going to live to see tomorrow. You redneck motherfucker," Bouchard threatened.

Jimmy pushed the barrel of his gun against his forehead. "Shut up and give me the keys."

Billy Joe hesitated for a brief moment before taking the keys from the ignition and tossing them on the seat as he was instructed.

"Atta boy, now give me the walkie–talkie that's sticking out of your pocket, and then slide out and step up against the car. You try any of that WCW shit with me and I'll show you who the *real* Undertaker is."

Billy laughed. "The Undertaker's in the WWF, dick–head."

"It figures you'd know that…and I'm the *redneck*, huh?" the sheriff replied.

After Jimmy frisked him, he cuffed one of his hands to a parking sign and the other to the door handle. He tossed Bouchard's walkie–talkie into his vest pocket and checked the handcuffs one more time. "Looks like you and your car aren't going anywhere for awhile. I'll be back in a few," he said as he walked toward the bank.

As soon as Jimmy opened the oak doors and stepped inside the bank, a hand grabbed hold of his collar and yanked him away from the entrance. He felt the point of a gun against his ribs. A group of hostages, guarded by a large man brandishing a semi–automatic weapon, was huddled on the floor about twenty feet to the sheriff's right. Anne Taggert wasn't one of them. Neither she nor the third gunman was anywhere in sight.

The man at the door was Kyle Peterson. He was a well–muscled former marine who served in the Gulf War. He stood four inches under six feet and weighed close to 225 pounds. Finding an ounce of fat on him was like trying to find a needle in a haystack. His brown hair was cut short, almost brush–cut short. His thick side–burns, goatee, and earrings, although in style, seemed out of character.

He'd been diagnosed with an Intermittent Explosive Disorder when he was seventeen. In lay terms, he had a short fuse. The anabolic steroids he was overdosing on at the time made a bad situation worse. His parents, desperately looking for help, shipped him off to bootcamp a week after his eighteenth birthday. Kyle had a promising future with the Marines until he got all liquored up one night and punched out his C.O. They sent him packing, dishonorable discharge in hand, a week later.

The man guarding the hostages was his second cousin, Danny Robinson. Robinson was a huge, towering man who never managed to get through elementary school. "Mildly retarded" was the label guidance counselors put on him–destined to pump gas for the rest of his life. "Dumb as a box of rocks" was the neighborhood's diagnosis. He was dumb as they come but intimidating as hell. A scraggly beard covered much of his ruddy face, including the long scar that ran from his earlobe to his chin, a souvenir from the two years he spent in Michigan's Ionia Maximum Correctional Facility. His long black hair was tucked up under a baseball cap. Both arms were littered with tattoos of naked woman, skulls, and snakes. A pinch of chewing tobacco was stuffed deep into his cheek.

"You're not going to be doing any banking today, pops. Get over there with the others," Peterson said gruffly. He shoved Jimmy forward, almost knocking him off his feet.

Jimmy turned his head ever so subtlety as he passed by the vault, catching a fleeting glimpse of his wife standing next to the third bank robber. The gunman, Michael Baker, had a semi–automatic pistol in his hand and an MP–5 assault rifle draped over his shoulder. Anne Taggert was stuffing stacks of hundred dollar bills into a large olive–green dufflebag as fast as she could, pausing every so often to wipe the tears from her face.

Danny Robinson used the barrel of his rifle, motioning for Jimmy to sit on the floor alongside the others. "What the fuck's taking so long?" he asked impatiently. Beads of sweat ran down his forehead and face, collecting on his collar.

"Relax, he'll be out soon. We're right on schedule," Peterson replied calmly. Jimmy slid the pistol from his pocket and placed it on the floor between his legs without either man noticing just as his wife and Baker emerged from the vault. She was walking a few steps in front of him. His pistol was pointed at her back and the dufflebag was slung over his shoulder.

Michael Baker didn't look like your typical criminal. Not the kind you see on the FBI's most wanted list. He was good–looking and well groomed. He was a little above average in stature and at least ten pounds underweight. His blonde hair was neatly layered. He was clean–shaven and fair skinned. Wire–rimmed glasses housed tinted lenses that hid deep blue eyes. He was thirty–one years–old but looked closer to twenty–five. He looked like the type of guy you hoped your daughter would meet.

Peterson was grinning from ear to ear. "What did I say, man? I told ya he'd be out soon," he gloated.

Anne Taggert's eyes lit up as she stepped past the last set of desks and noticed her husband sitting on the floor.

Jimmy shook his head back and forth just slightly enough for his wife to notice without alerting anyone else.

"Ahh, there's nothing like the smell of money in the morning," Baker said smugly. "It's been a pleasure doing business with you, folks. I hate to steal and run but I'm sure you'll understand."

"You want them in the vault?" Robinson asked.

Baker nodded, "yeah, put 'em in the hole and bring the car around."

Robinson stepped to the side and motioned for the hostages to move. "You heard the man. Let's go," he yelled.

Peterson pulled a walkie–talkie from his pocket and pressed the talk button. "Bring the car up—"

The walkie–talkie that Jimmy had stuffed into his pocket barked, echoing Peterson's words.

Baker dropped the dufflebag and spun sharply in Jimmy's direction. "What the fu—"

Jimmy grabbed Robinson by the collar, yanked him close, and put his pistol to his head. "Drop your rifle!" he yelled.

Peterson trained his pistol on Jimmy while Baker grabbed Anne Taggert by the neck and pulled her tight to his body. The barrel of his 9mm pistol was flush against her face and his arm was draped around her neck. Robinson eased his rifle to the floor.

"Let her go," Jimmy yelled.

"And if I don't?" Baker scowled.

"No one has to die here. Take the money and leave. No one will follow you. You have my word on it," Jimmy said.

Baker tightened his grip on Jimmy's wife. She could feel his hot breath on her neck. The stale smell of cigarette smoke clung to his clothes. His forearm pinched her throat, making it difficult to breathe. "Gee whiz, that's awful nice of you, old man. But in case you haven't noticed, you're outnumbered and outgunned. So why don't you put your gun down before I kill this bitch. I'll start with her and work my way through the others. It'll be a friggin' blood–bath in here when I'm through."

Jimmy pulled the gunman closer while keeping an eye on Peterson. The beads of sweat on Robinson's forehead formed little streams, which rolled down his face and soaked his shirt. "Do the smart thing. Take the money and leave."

"You didn't just happen to find that walkie–talkie on the sidewalk, did you? And that means our driver is likely to be incapacitated. So quit *fucking* with me and drop your gun. Do it or I'll pop her right now," Baker said, cocking the hammer on his pistol. His lips curled into a menacing smile.

Peterson took a couple of slow steps to the right, trying to get a cleaner line of sight, while Baker talked.

Anne Taggert was trembling. Her face was flushed and she was light–headed, so light–headed that she was close to fainting.

Jimmy looked into Baker's eyes. They were cold and penetrating. He knew he wasn't bluffing. He knew he was out of options and time. "I'll drop it if you take me instead of her."

Baker smiled. “I can live with that. Now drop your piece. I’m not asking again.”

Jimmy slowly laid his pistol on the desk and stepped back with his hands in the air.

Robinson lurched forward, grabbed his rifle, and jammed its butt sharply into Jimmy’s ribs, doubling him over. He followed the blow to the ribs with a swift uppercut that sent the sheriff sprawling across the floor. He stepped over him, straddling his chest, and put the rifle barrel to face. “You’re dead, cocksucker.”

Anne Taggert broke free of Baker’s grip and rushed to her husband. “NO…LEAVE HIM ALONE,” she screamed.

Robinson grabbed her with one hand and carelessly tossed her to the floor. She slid across the cold tile, tearing her blouse on the edge of a desk before crashing, headfirst, into a wooden post.

Jimmy knocked the rifle from Robinson’s hand and leg whipped him, sending him crashing to the ground. He sprang to his feet, leaped on top of him, and drew back his fist.

But Peterson stepped forward and put a gun to Jimmy’s head before he could land a blow.

Baker pulled Anne Taggert to her feet and shoved her toward the other hostages. “Get over there with the others, bitch.” He motioned to Peterson. “Check the bastard out. See what else he’s hiding.”

Anne glanced at her husband and reluctantly walked over to the other hostages while Peterson pulled Jimmy to his feet. “Let’s get that coat off and see what else you have tucked away in there, pops.”

Robinson gathered himself and collected his rifle. “You’re dead, motherfucker,” he muttered.

Jimmy slowly pulled the zipper down, exposing his badge and nametag.

“Shit. He’s a fucking cop,” Peterson announced.

Robinson jerked his head around. “What? You said all the cops would be gone. What’s he doing here?”

Baker turned toward Robinson. "Shut the fuck up." He looked at Peterson. "Keep an eye on the door."

Jimmy remained still with his arms up over his head.

Baker grabbed his coat and quickly went through the pockets. He pulled Billy Joe's pistol from a pocket. "Well, Sheriff…Taggert is it?" he asked as he bent forward and read Jimmy's nametag. "Taggert, that name sounds familiar. I swear I've—" He walked over to the sign above the teller station and smiled broadly.

Bank Manager–Mrs. Anne Taggert, was spelled out in large black letters.

"Coming to your wife's rescue like a knight in shining armor, huh, Officer Taggert? That's so friggin' touching. Isn't it, boys?"

"Yeah, a real tear–jerker. Get me a tissue will ya?" Peterson laughed.

Robinson wiped the sweat from his forehead and face. "Let's get out of here before more cops come," he said nervously.

Peterson chimed in, "I say we kill the prick."

"Put everyone in the vault except the sheriff and his wife," Baker ordered. "A man won't take chances…not when we've got his wife."

"Richie, this is Max…come in."

"Yeah, Max, what is it?"

"How far out are ya?"

"Less than ten. Any word from the Sheriff?"

"Nope, quieter than a church mouse since he went inside."

"Think I should head over there?"

"How far away is Steve?" Richie asked.

"He just checked in a minute ago…said he was turning onto Route 63. I figure he'll get there just about the same time as you."

"You better hang tight, Max. Jimmy can handle things. I'm really gonna push this bad boy now…I'll be there in five. Get Steve back on the horn. Tell him to take the dirt road that runs from five corners to

Route 16...it will shave three or four miles from his trip. Tell him to hurry."

Max clicked the microphone. "You got it, Richie."

❧ ❧ ❧

Baker turned to Jimmy. "So, Sheriff, how many men you got out there?"

"None, you called 'em both away on bogus deer–car accidents. Remember?"

Baker stepped forward and stared. "I'm going to take you at your word. We're going right out the front door. But if I see anyone wearing tin out there I'll cap your wife. If you're telling the truth this will all be over and you can go back to protecting this back–ass town. I'm sure Aunt Bea is whipping up an apple pie back home and Opie's fishing with Goober. You better pray I don't see Deputy Fife out there...she catches a bullet if I do."

No one's out there. You've got my word on it."

"Come on, let's get the fuck out of here. What are we waiting for?" Robinson pleaded.

"All right, we'll go. I'll lead and take the Sheriff's wife," Baker said. He picked up the dufflebag and tossed it to Robinson. "Here, you hang on to this and don't fucking drop it." He turned to Peterson. "You're in the middle. You take the Sheriff. Shoot him if he fucks with you."

Peterson looked at Jimmy and winked. "It would be a pleasure," he sneered.

Jimmy glanced at his wife. "It'll be all right," he said softly.

Cold air rushed into the bank as Baker opened the doors. The morning fog had lifted and the sun was shining bright. He cautiously stepped out onto the stone steps with Jimmy's wife pulled tight to his body, pausing for a moment to let his eyes adjust to the bright sunlight. He jammed his pistol deep into her ribs, and wrapped an arm tightly around her frail neck.

The town worker in the cherry picker was the first to notice. He let go of the street light cover he was holding. It crashed to the ground and exploded into a million pieces as he yelled down to the rest of the crew and pointed. Mark Coleman and his adolescent gang poked their heads around the corner and stared.

By now, the rest of the gunmen were outside. Baker was tight to the building, so tight his back scraped against the fieldstone facade as he crept along its perimeter. He was still using Anne Taggert as a shield. Peterson was close behind. One hand held a gun to Jimmy's head; the other had a firm grip on his collar. Robinson had the dufflebag strapped across his back. His head swiveled back and forth as he nervously scanned the streets for cops. Anne Taggert's face was wet with tears and her body trembled. Sam's pistol, tucked away in Jimmy's boot, scraped his ankle with each step he took.

Joe Morgan, one of the town workers, made the instinctive mistake of stepping towards them, carrying a five–foot two–by–four in one hand.

Baker raised his pistol without warning and fired, dropping Morgan before he took a second step. His body bounced when it hit the cold concrete and his bright orange jumpsuit quickly turned red. The sound of the shot wrapped itself around the leafless trees that lined the street. Its lingering echo filled the cool autumn air. A brown squirrel dropped an acorn and scurried into the safety of its nest.

Anne Taggert screamed, dropped to her knees, covered her head with her arms, and sobbed.

Jimmy struggled in vain to free himself from Peterson's grip. "You didn't have to shoot him you son–of–a–bitch!" he yelled.

"I know. But, I wanted to," Baker answered coldly. "Anyone else want to be a hero today. I've got plenty of bullets left," he yelled to the rest of the work crew. No one moved, not even to help Morgan. "I didn't think so. Now back off and go back to drinking your coffee and standing around with your thumbs up your ass." He jerked Jimmy's wife back to her feet and continued towards the car.

Peterson stepped forward to admire Baker's work. "What's all the fuss? He did your fucking town a favor. One less nigger to worry about," he said smiling.

⁂

Less than five blocks away, the switchboard in the Sheriff's Office lit up with 911 calls a few moments after Joe Morgan's body hit the ground. Max Wakefield took a 12–gauge shotgun and a box of shells from the gun rack, and rushed out the office door.

Max was book smart and a computer whiz but not a whole lot of help in the field. His five–foot four–inch frame carried two hundred plus pounds and the coke bottle lenses that covered his eyes still didn't afford him 20/20 vision. He had only shot his service revolver once in an undistinguished, sixteen–year career. And that was to put a deer out of its misery after being struck by a tractor–trailer on Route 16, the day after Christmas in '93. It took him two shots. The first just grazed the poor animal's head, making a bad situation worse.

⁂

Baker turned the corner, dragging Anne Taggert with him, and found Billy Joe still cuffed to the parking sign and door handle. "You stupid son–of–a–bitch. How the *fuck* did you let this yokel do that to you? You look like a friggin' scarecrow with your arms stretched out like that."

"He snuck up on me. I didn't see him coming. Someone must have tipped him off or something," Bouchard whimpered, looking like a dog with its tail between its legs.

Baker wiped his forehead with the back of his hand and stared coldly at Bouchard. "No one tipped him off, shithead. All you had was one simple job to do…just one fucking job and you screwed it up."

Jimmy turned his head and caught a glimpse of Max waddling down the sidewalk, staying tight to the buildings, holding a shotgun with both hands. It would have been comforting to him had it been Richie or Steve. Instead, he had a sinking feeling in the pit of his stomach.

Baker turned to Jimmy. "Give me the keys."

Jimmy reached in his pocket and tossed him a set of keys to the Bouchard's handcuffs.

"The *car* keys, asshole!"

"Let my wife go and—"

Baker shoved his pistol deep into the small of Anne Taggert's back and cocked the hammer. "No more games. Give me the keys. Do it now and she lives. Hesitate and she takes a trip to the morgue. It's your call."

Jimmy looked at Baker with an icy stare before turning the keys over. "You've got the keys now let her go," he demanded.

Max had made it to the cherry picker without being seen, which was an accomplishment in itself. He positioned the rifle barrel between a small groove in its orange metal frame and rested an elbow on its large tire. He was gasping to catch his breath as his heart thundered out of control. His shirt was soaked with sweat and a thick layer of condensation coated his glasses. Perspiration rolled off his face, dripping on the cold steel of the cherry picker. Joe Morgan's body lay on the ground less than twenty feet away. A thin crack in the concrete carried a steady stream of deep red blood to the curb, where it butted up against a newspaper box and collected into a large, macabre puddle. A faint wisp of steam rose from the puddle and disappeared into the crisp morning air.

The sidewalk and streets adjacent to the bank were barren now. People huddled in doorways and straddled corners, trying to stay clear of the impending melee. Every so often, Mark Coleman's head would jut out from behind a mailbox, looking like a turtle popping his head out of its shell.

Baker handed the keys to Robinson.

"Where the hell are Richie and Steve? They should be here by now," Jimmy wondered.

Max's hands were trembling as he slid the safety off and took aim.

Robinson walked to the driver side of the car and opened the door. He started to bend forward but stopped when he caught sight of the bright reflection off Max's glasses. "There's a fucking cop over there!" he yelled, drawing his rifle up to his chest and squeezing the trigger. Bullets bounced off the cherry picker and surrounding buildings, flooding the streets with ricochets.

Max's first two shots tore into Bouchard, killing him instantly. His head slumped forward until his chin rested on his chest. One arm was still pinned to the car door, the other to the parking sign.

Anne Taggert jerked forward, trying to free herself. Baker tightened his grip and dug the pistol deeper into her ribs.

Jimmy sent an elbow into Peterson's stomach, doubling him over. He turned sharply and kicked the pistol from his hand in one fluid motion.

Robinson returned Max's fire, using the car door for cover. Bullet shells cascaded from his rifle, littering the street at his feet. He paused just long enough to feed another clip into his hungry rifle.

Jimmy dove for the pistol. His body skidded on the cement as his fingertips stretched for its handle. He was only inches away when two bullets exploded on the sidewalk just a fraction of an inch from his hand. Chips of concrete flew up, peppering his face. Their sharp edges dug deep into his skin. He jerked his arm away and rolled over. Baker stepped forward, kicking the pistol to Peterson while holding Anne Taggert in one hand.

"GET IN THE CAR," he yelled to Peterson.

Max quickly emptied his shogun and switched to his service revolver. Bullets tattooed the cherry picker. Bits of rubber exploded off the tires.

Peterson jumped to his feet and took a step toward Jimmy, holding a pistol in his outstretched arm. "Kiss your ass goodbye, motherfucker," he yelled.

Jimmy reached for the gun he had tucked in his boot but was a split–second too slow.

Peterson's lips curled into an eerie smile as he cocked the hammer on his pistol and took aim at the Sheriff's head.

"NOOOO," Anne Taggert screamed at the top of her lungs.

A stray bullet from Max's service revolver found its mark a split–second later, tearing into Peterson's shoulder.

Richie's squad car turned the corner and skidded to a halt. He bolted from the car and laid down a line of fire while Max reloaded.

Baker threw Jimmy's wife to the ground and pulled Peterson to his knees, pushing him into the backseat. Robinson slid into the car and cranked the engine. Peterson recovered enough to spray the black and white with bullets as Baker jumped through the passenger side window.

Robinson revved the engine and threw the car in drive. It peeled away from the curb with Bouchard's bloody body still cuffed to the car door. His arm was ripped from its socket, tearing away at the shoulder. It swung wildly from the door handle, leaving a gruesome trail as the car screeched around the corner.

Jimmy lay on his back with Sam's revolver held firmly in his hands. He emptied its chambers with six quick pulls of the trigger.

Baker leaned out the window, pointed his assault rifle at Jimmy's wife, and squeezed the trigger. "Tell Aunt Bea to set one less plate at the dinner table," he sneered. His lips curled into a lifeless smile. His haunting laugh echoed in the alley.

Anne Taggert struggled to her feet as blood rushed from her body. She took two wobbly steps before falling forward into her husband's arms.

* * *

Jimmy held his dying wife, resting her head in his lap. The last breath left her body before she could utter a single word. The color ran from her face, leaving an ashen hue in its wake. His world stood still for a long, silent moment as shock grabbed hold of him. He sat on the cold sidewalk, paralyzed, covered in her blood, tears rolling down his face. He never heard Richie frantically calling for an ambulance on the police radio or Max's voice offering words of comfort. He never noticed the crowd of people closing in around him.

A block away, fifteen–year–old Mark Coleman lay next to his skateboard with a bullet lodged deep in his spine. His legs would never carry his weight again. Joe Morgan's body lay lifeless and cold, his hand still clutching the two–by–four.

CHAPTER 5

Both funerals were on Tuesday. Joe Morgan's was in the morning, followed by Anne Taggert's two hours later. Darien closed down for the day and the flags at the town hall and post office were lowered to half–mast. There wasn't a soul in town that didn't attend at least one of the services. Most attended both. Storm clouds hung over the county most of the day, laying down a good six inches of snow by noon. Strong gusts of arctic air, pouring down from Canada, whipped the snow into drifts and kept the plows busy well into the night.

Jimmy spent the remainder of the week and weekend with his children and grandchildren, seeking comfort that never came. The last of his family left after lunch on Sunday. He was back at work the following day.

"I ain't never seen the Sheriff like that," Deputy Steve Thompson said, remembering how Jimmy looked at the cemetery. He leaned back, deep into his chair, with the heel of his boot resting on the edge of his desk. One leg was draped on top of the other, his arms were folded across his muscular chest. Jimmy sat all alone in his office, looking out the window with a blank stare on his face. A picture of his wife, set in a brass frame and surrounded by pictures of his grandchildren, sat on the corner of his desk.

Thompson had celebrated his ten–year anniversary with the Darien Police Department the weekend before the shooting. He was a good–natured farm boy, half the size of a house. He had been the most highly recruited high school football player in the state his senior year, and had offers to play from every major college program in the nation. But his dad lost a leg to cancer in the fall of '86 so he stayed home to help run the farm. His father passed away two years later and his mom was forced to sell the farm. Steve walked into the Sheriff's Office looking for work and Jimmy hired him a week later.

"I never saw that look in his eyes before. I don't know if I've ever seen that look in anyone's eyes, to tell you the truth, Richie. It kinda scared me. Whatta you suppose he's gonna do now? Do you think he'll still retire?"

Richie Atwater looked back over his shoulder and stared at the Sheriff for a long while before answering. He methodically rolled a toothpick from one corner of his mouth to the other and back again. He ran his hand over the top of his head, letting his fingertips massage his short bristles of brown hair.

Richie didn't look much like a cop. He was tall and wiry, but tough as nails. Occasionally, out–of–towners, with too much to drink would make the mistake of taking a swing at him at the DWI roadblocks he worked every Friday night. They usually ended up flat on their backs, nursing a black eye or broken jaw. Richie's fuse wasn't short but it didn't burn too long either.

"A bunch of years back, about a year after I joined the force, I took the wife and kids on a vacation. We went down to the Magic Kingdom…stayed in one of the hotels inside the place. Can't think of the name right now," Richie said, scratching his head. "Anyway, I went down to the bar for a cold one while Margaret took a shower and the kids took a nap. I'm sitting at the bar, tipping back a few cold ones, watching a ballgame, when this guy next to me starts jawing with me. He was an Italian guy by the name of Masseti, a shoe salesman, I think. I mention that I'm from Darien. Now, you know that no one outside this county ever knows where the hell Darien is…no one 'cept this guy. Then, he leans forward and asks me if I know a fella by the name of Jimmy Taggert."

"Get out!" Thompson said, raising an eyebrow.

Richie raised his right hand in the air. "I swear it's true. As God is my witness."

"How did he know the Sheriff?"

"Said he and Jimmy served in 'Nam. They were in the same platoon."

Thompson turned and studied Jimmy for a moment. "I never knew he was in 'Nam."

Richie took the toothpick from his mouth, flicked it in the trashcan, and continued. "I've known the Sheriff for close to twenty years, and he's only mentioned the war once in all that time. Jimmy's like that though. He don't like to talk about that stuff much at all. Keeps it real private. Anyway, getting back to what I was saying. This guy tells me that Jimmy was a living legend in the 82nd airborne." He paused just long enough to stick a fresh toothpick in the corner of his mouth. "You're too young to remember Bobby Ryan, aren't you?"

Thompson nodded. "I heard he died in the war. I met his brother a few times. He and my uncle used to pal around."

"Yeah, well, Jimmy and Bobby Ryan were best of friends, tighter than two peas in a pod. Wherever you seen one, you seen the other. Did everything together, including joining the army and getting shipped off to 'Nam. This guy told me that Bobby got ambushed by the Vietcong one day. Said they butchered him real bad, even cut off his ear, left him to die in the jungle."

Thompson cringed. "They cut off his ear?"

"Yeah, cut it clean off. Bobby died in Jimmy's arms a couple of minutes after they found him. Masseti told me that Jimmy lost it.

Said he stayed in the jungle that night, all alone…hunting down the bastards like a pack of rabid dogs."

Thompson swung his legs down from the desk and leaned forward. "What happened?"

"He killed everyone of 'em. Masseti said they went back out on patrol a week later and stumbled on the bodies…or what was left of 'em. One of the pricks was missing both his legs. Another had his throat slit from one end to the other. Bullets had ripped another two to shreds."

"He killed four men by himself?"

"Yep, killed all four of 'em without so much as a scratch on himself."

Steve leaned back and ran his fingers through his hair. "Holy shit!" he said.

Atwater looked back at his boss and shook his head. "The Sheriff won't retire, not with those scumbags on the loose. He won't turn in his badge 'til they're rotting in jail or dead. Those bastards don't have any idea what they're in for…no fucking idea at all."

Max Wakefield stepped away from the window. He had a cup of coffee in one hand and half of a cream–filled doughnut in the other. A ring of powdered sugar coated his puffy lips. "Hey, the snow's finally letting up," he announced, before cramming the rest of the doughnut in his mouth.

"It's about time. I can't remember ever getting this much snow so early in the year. I bet we got over two feet since it started…maybe more," Atwater commented.

Jimmy stepped out of his office and filled his coffee mug for the third time. "Any word on the getaway car, Max? How fucking hard can it be to find a black Cadillac with an arm handcuffed to the door handle?"

"Nothing so far, Chief. Nothing at all. I sent alerts to Pennsylvania, Ohio, and Canada, and haven't heard squat yet. It's like they disappeared into thin air."

"They must have ditched the car and squeezed through the roadblock somehow. Maybe they split up," Thompson added.

Jimmy topped off his coffee with a tablespoon of cream. "Any reports from hospitals, Max? The guy that caught one in the shoulder would have needed some medical attention."

"I've contacted every hospital, clinic, and doctor's office within 200 miles, and came up empty."

"Check all the veterinarians too," Jimmy grumbled. "What do we know about the driver?"

"The FBI jacket on him is thick as a brick. He's a piece of work by the name of Billy Joe Bouchard. Grew up in the French Quarter, not too far from Bourbon Street. His dad was a long shoreman who pissed away most of his paycheck in riverboat casinos and whorehouses. What little money he brought home was used to feed his mom's rather large appetite for Jack Daniels. Not exactly Ozzie and Harriet types, huh?"

"Billy Joe spent his formative years on the streets. He's been arrested a shit–load of times. A few for assault, a few for breaking and entering, forgery, and robbery. Typical thug stuff. He did time in Louisiana for rape and attempted murder a few years back. Seems a Saints cheerleader ended up in the wrong redneck bar on the wrong night. Billy Joe waited for her in the parking lot while he polished off half a quart of Southern Comfort. He threw her in his truck and took her to a loading dock on the edge of the Mississippi. The report says he beat her unconscious after raping and sodomizing her for more than three hours. She ended up with a fractured skull, broken ribs and a punctured lung. The bastard bit one of her nipples completely off and burned the other with a cigarette. Her body was more black and blue than flesh colored when the asshole was finished. Report says he was about to dump her in the river when a night watchman came along. Billy Joe took off but not before the watchman caught his plate number. Bouchard cut a deal with the DA and plea–bargained down. The prick was back on the streets less than three years later. There's also an outstanding federal warrant for him. Seems he's been linked to some of our country's finer militia and white supremacist groups."

"What's the federal warrant for?" Jimmy asked.

"He's wanted as a material witness in the theft of plastic explosives from a U.S. military base," a well–dressed man said, as he entered the room and took off his cashmere overcoat. He brushed the snow off of it before carefully draping it over the back of a chair. His double–breasted, dark blue suit was nicely fitted to his broad shoulders. He gently tapped the snow from his Italian–leather wingtip shoes and stepped further into the room. His well–groomed hair was a light shade of gray. A thin mustache lined his upper lip. He was a hair under six feet tall. Jimmy noticed his gait was a bit uneven.

The station mascot, a collie–lab mix by the name of Dillon, rose from a long nap to give the stranger a thorough sniff. He went up one leg and down the other before returning to the comfort of his sheepskin rug, and warmth of the radiator. "Do you know where I can pick up a pair of boots? I wasn't expecting this much damn snow. We don't get this much in D.C. in a decade and a half…maybe longer."

"Who the hell are you?" Jimmy asked.

"Mitchell Corey," he replied, extending his well manicured hand. "I'm with the FBI. Stationed in Quantico. I'm the Deputy Director of the D.T.U."

Jimmy stepped forward to shake his hand. "And what exactly is the D.T.U., Agent Corey?"

"I prefer Mitchell, if you don't mind? You must be Sheriff Taggert. Please accept my condolences for the loss of your wife," Corey said.

Jimmy swallowed hard and offered a slight nod. His lip quivered slightly. *The loss of your wife.* The words rattled around aimlessly in his head. Their hollow echo reverberated in distant regions of his brain, unable to take hold—unable to find a home in his consciousness.

"D.T.U. is an abbreviation for the Domestic Terrorist Unit. It's a relatively new branch of the Bureau's. We've grown quite a bit over the last several years, thanks to the Oklahoma City bombing and the Unabomber. A sign of the times, unfortunately."

"I'm assuming our fingerprint search for Mr. Bouchard set off one of your trip wires and that's why you're vacationing with us this morning. Excuse me if I sound a bit rude or out of line, but why would the Bureau fly a Deputy Director all the way from Washington to Darien for a corpse? Why not send an agent from the local office in Buffalo?" Jimmy asked pointedly.

Corey rubbed his hands together and hunched his shoulders. "That coffee sure smells good. It's cold out there. I could use a cup to warm me up, if you don't mind. My flight left at seven o'clock. It's been a long morning."

"Max, get Mr. Corey a cup, will you?"

"Thanks, Sheriff. A little cream, no sugar, if you don't mind, Max?" Corey said. A slight smile crept up on his face. He slid a chair out from under a table and sat down. Jimmy introduced Atwater and Thompson as each pulled up a chair and joined them. A narrow slice of sunlight squeezed through the curtains and landed on the floor by the FBI agent's feet. It was the first bit of sunshine Darien had seen in more than four days. "I didn't come all this way for Bouchard. I'm looking for the man he was with. A man by the name of Michael Baker." Agent Corey pulled an envelope from his vest pocket and laid a collection of mug shots on the desk. "That's Michael Baker," he said pointing to one of the photos. Baker was much younger in the photo, by five or six years at least. His hair was long, tied back in a ponytail. His lips were curled into an eerie smile and his eyes were narrow and cold.

Jimmy stared at the photo of Baker as it lay on the desk. His eyes narrowed and pulse jumped. A knot formed in the pit of his stomach. The muscles in his jaws were rigid, and his fists were clenched. A flashback took him to the corner outside the bank. He could see the smirk on Baker's face as he casually squeezed the trigger. His haunting laugh echoed in his head as he held his wife for the last time.

Jimmy struggled to stay in control. He could feel his emotions welling up, boiling over inside–desperately seeking to escape in a maddening rush. He choked back the tears, closed his eyes, and swallowed hard. It had been thirty years since he had felt such deep, penetrating pain. It had been thirty years since his best friend was butchered in the jungles of 'Nam.

A long moment passed before he mustered enough composure to speak. "Looks like we're after the same man." His voice was distant and flat. He pulled two other mug shots from the agent's collection. "These two were with him."

Corey laid the three photos side by side. "Kyle Peterson and Danny Robinson," he explained, massaging his chin with a forefinger and thumb. "They've been with Baker for a while now. Peterson's been teamed up with him for more than five years, and Robinson's in his junior year. Bouchard was in his rookie season, so to speak. He took over for Baker's half–brother after we nabbed him. He's doing twenty–five–to–life at Attica for armed robbery and attempted murder."

Max laid a cup of coffee down on the desk next to Corey and pointed at Peterson's photo. "That's the one that caught a bullet in the shoulder. We found a pretty good–sized trail of blood leading up to their car."

"Baker won't take him to a hospital or doctor's office. Not even if the poor bastard's bleeding to death," Corey commented.

Jimmy picked up Baker's mug shot and studied it for a moment. "Tell me what you know about this son–of–a–bitch."

"He's pretty much your typical sociopath…angry white male with a photographic memory and an IQ that's through the roof. He has a doctorate from M.I.T. in engineering but can't hold down a job to save his life. Seems to have a problem with authority, thinks he's smarter than everyone else. His parents divorced when he was six.

His dad moved out–of–state a year later when his company folded up their tents and took the jobs down south. He eventually lost contact with his father. You know the story, dad meets another woman, starts a new family, doesn't have the time or the money for his son anymore. His mom remarried a few years later and had another kid. Same thing happened there. Michael's sitting the bench. He's second string all over again."

"He buried himself in books, closed the world out for awhile. He got straight A's all through school. Ended up with a full–ride to M.I.T. Great grades…the kid's quiet as hell…doesn't bother a soul…doesn't take drugs. Mom thinks he's doing just fine, exactly what her son wants her to think, exactly what he wants everyone to think. Meanwhile, her sweet little boy is holed up in the basement conducting experiments on the neighborhood's cats and dogs. Textbook psychopath stuff…cutting the eyes out of dogs and cats. Trying to sew the cat's eye into the dog's head. Seeing how long it takes a dog to bleed to death after stabbing it with a screwdriver. Seeing if cats really *do* have nine lives. You know, the usual insane shit found in the Psycho's R Us Handbook." Mitchell Corey paused to take a drink of coffee. It was lukewarm and stale. *Day–old coffee tastes better,* he thought.

"What do guys like Peterson and Baker have in common? How'd they hook up?" Jimmy asked.

Corey forced another mouthful a coffee down and continued. "Peterson and Baker went to the same high school. A small school south of Detroit. Peterson was a hell of an athlete, but piss poor with the books. Baker got him through school in exchange for protection and an opportunity to hangout with the *cooler* kids. You've probably seen that same type of arrangement when you were in high school…everybody has."

Max nodded. "I remember this kid by the name of—"

"Those relationships usually fizzle out after high school," Jimmy interrupted. "What happened here? Baker doesn't strike me as the type who gives a rat's ass about fitting in with anyone or anything. What's important in high school usually doesn't amount to a hill of beans in the real world. It wouldn't take someone like Baker long to figure that out."

"It's actually quite simple, Sheriff. Greed…greed keeps them together. Baker supplies the brains. The banks they've selected have been well researched, escape routes, timing, security, and most importantly—cash on hand. All have been in areas that are close to the Canadian border. Baker's sharp…and ruthless. He doesn't make mistakes. Peterson kicks in the muscle and manpower. He's got a lot of connections. They've robbed twelve banks, including yours. We figure they've hauled in about two and a half million so far, and we think they're planning something big. Maybe in the five million dollar range."

"Sounds like your run–of–the–mill bank robbers to me, Agent Corey. Why would the D.T.U. be interested in thieves?" Atwater asked.

Corey loosened his tie and unbuttoned his collar. "Good question, Deputy. Some of the money they've stolen has been linked to rather large purchases of explosives from oversea dealers and domestic militia groups. Bouchard was heavily vested in the latter. Peterson's been on the fringes of some splinter groups of the Michigan Militia. We don't know if he's a player or just working them as contacts."

"Didn't you say Bouchard was wanted on a federal warrant for stealing explosives from a military base? Why steal 'em? Why not just buy the damn stuff? They certainly have the cash. Why take the risk?" Jimmy asked.

"The shit that was stolen can't be bought. Not even on the black market…not yet anyway. It's a new class of plastic explosives called '*Generation X*.' It's top secret, lightweight, and extremely powerful. It makes C–4 seem like a friggin' firecracker. It also has the rather unique property of being able to be melted down and transported in its liquid form. And unlike nitro…it's completely stable. It takes a couple of hours to set before it's volatile. Terrorists would love to get their hands on it because it's virtually undetectable. Hell, you could put in a thermos and walk into the White House without a Secret Service agent giving you a second look."

Jimmy slid the mug shots closer. "And you don't have any idea what they're planning on doing with this '*Generation X*' shit...do you?"

Corey hung his head. "Not a stinkin' clue," he admitted. He brought the cup of coffee to his mouth and took a swig. He winced and shook his head, spitting most of it back into the cup a second later. "No offense, Max, but this is some of the worst coffee I've ever had. What the hell's in this stuff?"

Thompson laughed. "I stopped drinking it. It's bad...really fucking bad coffee!"

"I don't know. I kind of like it. It's got a certain kick to it," Jimmy said.

Max took a long drink from his mug. "Ahhhh...is that good or what! Hell, you boys don't have any taste. They pay big bucks for coffee like this in the city. It's designer java. You have to have a little class to appreciate it. I could probably open a shop there. I bet I'd have to turn people away, the lines would be so long."

"More like you'd have to *bury* the people," Atwater joked.

Charlie Adams stepped out of the cold, carrying the Sheriff's mail in one hand and a dog biscuit in the other. "Son–of–a–gun, it's colder than a witch's tit out there, fellas." Charlie was bundled up in all the Post Office cold weather gear he could muster. His battleship–gray parka with the blue stripe running up the sleeves was pulled tight to his windblown face. A bright red scarf was wrapped tightly around his neck. Matching pants were tucked deep into his favorite thermal–lined hunting boots and his electric socks were cranking. Charlie laid the mail on the front desk, slid his hood down, and tossed the biscuit over to where Dillon was curled up. "I swear I'm moving south the day I retire. Thirty–three years of delivering mail in this crap is enough," he whined.

"Every winter you start yapping about moving south, Charlie. You're just like the rest of us…lifers," Atwater snickered. "They'll bury you here in Darien. Right next to the three mailmen we had before you."

"There's where you're wrong, Deputy know–it–all. I'll be sunning myself on the pearly white beaches of Florida with one of those fancy drinks in my hand while you got your skinny ass backed up to a pot belly stove just to keep it from freezing off. Yes, sir, no more snow shoveling for me in another two years. Just you wait and see." Charlie was grinning from ear to ear, happy to get the last word for a change. "Hey, Max, old–buddy, can you spare a cup of brew for your favorite postal employee?"

"Sure can, Charlie. Luck's on your side this morning. I just finished brewing a pot. It's got your name on it. Glad to see someone appreciates a good cup of java."

Thompson rolled his eyes. "Poor old Charlie's gonna be on his *side* if he drinks a pot of that swill."

Atwater put his finger down his throat, pretending to puke.

Jimmy laughed loudly. It was the first good laugh he had since his wife died. And it felt good.

"Hey, Sheriff."

"Yeah, Charlie."

"Are the Ryans' out of town?"

Jimmy turned sharply. "Not that I'm aware. There's a service for Bobby the day after tomorrow. Mrs. Ryan didn't mention she was going anywhere. Why?"

"They haven't touched their mail since last week. Their box is full. Can't cram no more in it. Damn junk mail is a bitch this time of year. Anytime they go out of town they call and ask me to hold up on the mail 'til they get back. Ain't like 'em to leave without calling."

Jimmy grabbed his coat and gloves. "What size shoe do you wear, Agent Corey?"

"Eleven. Why?"

"Good, same size as me. I've got a spare set of boots in the truck. You can use 'em 'til you get a chance to pick up a pair. Come on, we're going to swing by the Ryans' place. It's probably nothing, but I want to make sure."

CHAPTER 6

The last picture ever taken of Bobby Ryan sat in a collection of family photos on top of the mahogany mantle in the Ryans' living room. Bobby was sitting in the driver's seat of a Jeep, holding a bottle of Iron City beer in one hand while flashing the peace sign with the other. One of his long legs rested on the hood of the Jeep, his boot dangled freely in the air. A rifle hung from his shoulder and a cigarette was tucked behind his ear. His face, thick with freckles, sported his familiar toothy grin.

Jimmy Taggert had taken the picture in the summer of '68, a day before Bobby died.

Nattie Ryan deftly wrapped a fresh bandage tight to Peterson's shoulder and fixed it with the last of her surgical tape. The bullet had passed cleanly through, narrowly missing his collarbone and carotid artery. She stepped on the red and white tin trashcan's foot pedal and tossed a spent bandage in it as the lid popped open. It landed, with a thud, on top of a pile of blood–soaked bandages. "The bleeding's stopped and the wound doesn't look infected. He can travel now," she announced, looking Michael Baker squarely in the eyes. "You said you'd leave once it was safe to travel." There was more anger than fear in her voice. "There's a winter storm heading this way. Supposed to be a bad one. You might not be able to get out of here if you wait much longer."

"If I didn't know better, I'd swear you're trying to get rid of us, Nattie. Ed, what do you think? Think your wife's trying to get rid of us?" Baker snickered.

Ed Ryan stared straight ahead and didn't answer. His teeth were tightly clenched. His lower lip quivered. The slight squint of his eyes conveyed a deep seething anger. His thoughts turned to the loaded, double–barrel shotgun he kept hidden in the back of his bedroom closet. He had two shots for three men. He knew at age 83, he was no longer a match for thirty year–old men, especially men as powerful as Robinson and Peterson. He was in desperate need of a plan and quickly running out of time.

Baker lifted himself off the living room sofa and sauntered over to where Nattie stood. "I agree with you, Ed. She's a bit rude this morning. Probably that time of the month…on the rag," he said, and winked. "Looks like you'll be holding your own tonight, pops."

Mrs. Ryan took a step back. "You best be getting out of town before Sheriff Taggert gets a hold of you. He'll track you down like dogs for killing his wife. Won't stop 'til he finds you. Mark my words, he'll catch up with you all right. And when he does—"

"And when he does, I'll kill him like I killed that whore wife of his. If your Sheriff was so high and mighty how come he let his wife die? I'll tell you why. Because he's a fucking loser! A loser Sheriff for a loser town. I bet Darien's theme song is from '*Deliverance.*' You probably sell pictures of some retarded, buck–toothed, banjo playing kid, whose father and uncle are the same person, at your local five and dime. He's probably the Mayor's son. You're nothing but a bunch of dentally challenged, back–ass farmers who never got past the third grade. You're living in a century that's passed you by…only you're too incredibly stupid to realize it."

Baker stepped forward, pinning Nattie against the wall. His eyes were narrow and cold. A deep rage rumbled in the pit of his stomach, bubbling up through his veins.

Ed Ryan jumped up and rushed to help his wife. He took less than five steps before Robinson snared him and slammed his frail body to the floor, cracking a rib and fracturing his hip.

"The FBI's looking for me. They have been for years. But they haven't caught me…haven't even come close. Do you know why, Mrs. Ryan?" Baker asked angrily, spit flying from his lips.

The stench of alcohol flooded Nattie's nostrils, growing more pungent with every word he barked. She closed her eyes and turned her head away. *Please get us through this, Lord,* she prayed.

"Leave her alone, you bastard," Ed Ryan yelled, ignoring the sharp, cutting pain that came with each breath.

"Shut the fuck up, old man," Robinson barked, placing his foot over Ed Ryan's throat and pressing down.

Peterson sat on the sofa and laughed.

"BECAUSE I'M SMARTER THAN THEM! SMARTER THAN ALL OF THEM COMBINED!" Baker yelled at the top of his lungs. He took a step back, stared at her, and spoke after a long pause. "That's why they'll never catch me. Not the FBI, not the State Police, and certainly not Taggert." He turned toward Robinson. "Let the old man up. Maybe Nattie's right, maybe we've worn out our welcome. What do you say, Ed? Wanna go check out that Chevy Impala that's sitting in your barn? I'll trade you a shiny black Cadillac for it. It's a good deal. The Caddy's only got 125,000 miles…even comes with an arm attached to the door. You won't have a problem finding it in the parking lot. It'll stick out like a sore thumb," Baker howled. "It'll be quite a conversation piece at bingo. Don't you think? Hell, I'd give my right arm for a car like that."

"Gives a whole to meaning to the phrase '*lending a hand*' huh?" Peterson chimed in from the couch.

"I think you should stay here, Nattie. Ed and I can haggle over the price. It's a *guy* thing. You wouldn't be interested," Baker said, motioning for Peterson to keep an eye on her.

Robinson hoisted a grimacing Ed Ryan to his feet.

"I just need to get my jacket. It's in the bedroom closet," the old man said softly.

"Sure thing, pops. Wouldn't want you to catch a cold out there. You need to stay healthy so you can collect Social Security for another twenty years. Collect it long enough so there won't be any left for the rest of us," Baker jeered.

Ed Ryan trotted to the bedroom. His heart was thundering under his shirt, feeling like it was going to explode through his chest. Adrenaline flooded his aged body. A sharp, penetrating pain cut into his lungs with each breath he took. *Stay calm. Stay calm. Stay calm*, he said to himself over and over again. But he couldn't. He hoped Nattie would run as soon as he fired the shotgun. *At least let me get a couple of the bastards. At least let Nattie get away,* he prayed.

Nattie Ryan watched her husband disappear into the back bedroom. Outside, a light snow began falling. It floated down, past the windows, melting as it hit the ground. She wondered if this was the year she'd be spending Christmas with Bobby.

CHAPTER 7

The Ryans' lived in a small farmhouse on Route 16, about a quarter mile east of the Route 39 overpass. A steady north wind blew across open fields, churning up the snow and spilling it back onto the road. Jimmy downshifted and switched to four–wheel drive. Deep ruts in the snow–covered road tugged at his tires, threatening to propel the pickup deep into the three–foot high snow banks that lined the winding country road. Each time the drifts jerked his tires he would ease the truck back onto the road, being careful not to overcompensate and send it careening across the centerline.

"Christ! Is it always this nasty?" Agent Corey asked nervously. He reached across his waist, checking his seatbelt for a second time. "I don't suppose this truck happens to have passenger–side airbags. Does it?"

Jimmy laughed. "You folks don't see too much of the white stuff down in D.C...do ya? Hell, this ain't bad. You shoulda seen it the day before yesterday. You couldn't see your hand in front of your face; wind was blowing so damn hard. Snow was coming down...had to be three or four inches an hour, maybe more."

"Lake effect snow's a bitch. Erie ain't frozen over yet. It's a friggin' snow making machine this time of the year. Arctic air crossing over a wide–open lake that's a dozen degrees warmer is a recipe for disaster. You should have been here during the blizzard of '77. Now *that* was a snowstorm! Drifts were up to rooftops in spots. You couldn't leave your house. The damn town was closed down for more than a week and a half." Jimmy glanced at Corey and smiled. "A whole lot of babies were born nine months later. A regular bumper crop that year all right."

Suddenly a deep rut caught the truck's tires, forcing the pickup hard into the snowy shoulder. Jimmy quickly jerked the wheel to the left before the truck was pulled further off the road. Its backend fishtailed, crossing the centerline. An eighteen–wheeler, heading in the opposite direction and carrying a full load of lumber, was barreling towards them. Agent Corey threw his arms in front of his face and turned away. Jimmy calmly turned into the skid and righted the pickup a split–second before the truck rushed by. A thick blanket of road spray, thrown from the truck's tires, covered Jimmy's windshield for a few seconds until his wipers pushed the slush away.

"Damn! That was close," the Sheriff said, and smiled. He wiped his forehead with the back of his hand. "That gets the heart pumping…almost as much as Max's coffee. Don't you think?"

Corey was white as a ghost. "Is the house much further?" he asked.

Jimmy laughed. "It's up just past the next hill. Two miles from here."

"Back at your office you mentioned that there was a service for Bobby the day after tomorrow. Was he related to the Ryans?" Corey asked.

Jimmy glanced at the FBI agent and hesitated before answering. "Bobby was their son…and my best friend. He did three tours in Vietnam in the late sixties." He paused again and stared straight ahead. "His name's etched on *The Wall* in your city, along with the rest of the men who gave their lives for this country."

An uncomfortable moment passed before either man said a word.

"I was *in country* about the same time," Corey said, breaking the silence. "I was a chopper pilot for the better part of three tours. We ran into some heavy shit there. Had VC coming out our ass at times. I left a lot friends back there, too. I pass by the Vietnam Memorial every day on my way to the office. The truth of the matter is that I've only been there once. It brings back too many memories, mostly bad. Sometimes it's best to let the memories rest in peace. Just like the dead."

"Is that where you got your limp?"

Corey turned and looked at the Sheriff with surprise. "You don't miss much. Do you? I didn't think it was that noticeable."

"It's not. I've been a cop for thirty years. I notice things."

"Do you mind if I ask you a personal question, Sheriff?"

Jimmy shook his head. "Fire away."

"I pulled your jacket before I came up here. Nothing personal…standard operating procedure. You had quite an impressive record in 'Nam, two Purple Hearts and a Congressional Medal of Honor. It also said that you turned down recommendations for a promotion from your commanding officers on at least four occasions and—"

Jimmy interrupted. "And you want to know why."

"Yeah. You seem comfortable with command. Why not take the stripes. God knows you earned them."

"For a couple of reasons. I wasn't planning on making a career of the military. It wasn't the life I was looking for. Not my cup of tea, as they say. So moving up the ranks didn't mean a whole lot to me." Jimmy slid the truck into second gear and started up the last hill before the Ryans' farm. "But the main reason I turned down the offers was that I didn't want to be responsible for sending some kid fresh out of bootcamp to his death. I knew that dying went with the territory. I made my peace with God over there and was prepared to go if he decided it was my time. But I didn't want any part of playing God. I couldn't have lived with myself if some 18 year–old kid, barely old enough to shave, got himself killed because I sent him out on point or recon." He turned and looked at Corey. "That's why I told 'em to keep their stripes."

Jimmy's truck cleared the crest of the hill and the two men caught their first glimpse of Ryans' farmhouse. It was set on the southeast corner of their property. 320 acres of plush farmland bordered by Cazanovia Creek on the north end and the Route 400 expressway to the south. The farmhouse was set a good fifty yards off the road. An Amish style barn was a stone's throw to its right. The farmhouse, white with black shutters, was a two–story colonial that had been built a few years before the start of the Civil War. A massive field-stone chimney, that rose at least twenty feet beyond the roof, covered much of the left side of the house and stood in sharp contrast to the sea of white surrounding the property.

"Doesn't look like anyone's home. The driveway hasn't been plowed and the chimney's quiet. Maybe the mailman was right," Agent Corey noted.

Jimmy pulled over and slid the truck into park. A foot and a half of virgin snow buried the driveway. "Ed Ryan clears that driveway on a regular basis. He's got a plow rigged up to his tractor. Made it himself. It'd cut through this like butter. He does his neighbor's driveways a mile and a half in either direction, too. He loves driving that old tractor. His wife swears he spends more time on than off of it. I always see him tooling around on that thing with his headphones on, listening to Rush Limbaugh…happier than a pig in shit." Jimmy's smile turned into a laugh. "He's a character all right. Stubborn as the day is long. But he'd give you the shirt off his back if you asked. He's good people…*real* good people."

"What do you want to do?" Corey asked.

"They wouldn't miss Bobby's service, come hell or high water. Something ain't right. I feel it in my bones." The Sheriff pulled his gloves tight and slid his hat on. "There's too much snow in the driveway for this old heap. We'd get hung up before we were ten yards deep. Looks like we'll have to hike it from here," he said as he opened the door and climbed outside. He greeted the cold wind with a grimace.

The snow was knee high and tightly packed. The kind of snow that's good for making snowballs—the kind of snow that breaks your back shoveling it. The two men trudged through it, single file, with the Sheriff leading the way.

"I don't see any cars," Corey observed. Wisps of vapor floated from his mouth as his breath clashed with the cold morning air.

"They have a red pickup truck and an old Chevy Impala. They usually keep 'em in the barn during the winter. We'll look into that once we check on the house."

A blanket of snow covered half of the whitewashed slatted fence that lined one side of the driveway. A row of white maple trees, their branches bowed under the weight of the snow, ran from the road to the edge of the house on the opposite side of the driveway. A dense row of icicles collected along the eves. Their massive spikes hung down past the window tops.

"Son–of–a–bitch, I've got goddamn snow in my boot," Corey complained as he plodded through the drifts. "It's friggin' cold!"

Jimmy laughed. "Could be worse."

"How so?"

"Could be down your pants. That'd send a shiver down your spine. A whole bottle full of Viagra wouldn't help then."

"We haven't reached the house yet. Don't jinx me," Corey said laughing.

Half of the porch steps were under the snow line. Jimmy freed his leg from the snow's wintry grasp and stretched for the first visible step. The wooden stairs groaned under his weight as he lifted the rest of his body out of the snow. Agent Corey followed suit and both men were standing at the Ryans' front door a moment later. Jimmy checked the windows after his first two knocks went unanswered.

"Curtains are drawn tight, can't see a blessed thing in there," he announced.

"It's your call. What do you want to do?" Corey asked.

Jimmy reached under his coat and liberated his pistol. "Something's wrong. Let's go in." He removed a key from under the painted milk can on the porch and slid it into the lock. "It's a small town," he said.

Corey smiled. "I hadn't noticed."

The front door swung stiffly on brass hinges that squeaked loudly, echoing throughout the house. The porcelain doorknob bumped into the plaster wall with a hollow thud.

"Anyone home? Nattie...Ed? It's Jimmy...Jimmy Taggert."

An eerie silence answered back...drawing them inside.

Jimmy entered the house first, followed closely by Corey. Each brandished a semi–automatic pistol in their outstretched arms—safeties off. Sunlight flooded the gloomy foyer, throwing shadows against the darkened wall. Snow slid from their clothes, ponding on the black and white checkered linoleum. The two men inched forward, their eyes darting everywhere, and ears straining to catch the lightest of sounds. The foyer ended at the kitchen's edge. Dirty dishes, pots, and pans were stacked two feet high in the sink. Empty cans of beer, some crushed, littered the tile countertop. An assortment of condiments was strewn across the kitchen table, along with a stack of old newspapers. Two mugs, brimming with cigarette butts and ashes, were abandoned on the stove. The house was silent except for the gentle humming of the refrigerator.

Mrs. Ryan would have never left the house looking like this, Jimmy thought. *Not in a million years.* He gripped his pistol a little tighter. His palms were thick with sweat and his heart was pounding. Frosty breath billowed from his lungs. The floor creaked with each step he took. A flickering light, coming from underneath the living room door, caught his eye.

Jimmy stood at one side of the closed door, Agent Corey at the other, hugging the wall. Light danced back and forth across the threshold. The Sheriff used his fingers to silently count to three before slowly pushing the door into the room.

The FBI agent cocked the hammer of his gun, squatted down and drew a deep breath. "Let's do it," he whispered.

Jimmy nodded slightly and carefully leaned into the room, peering around the door. A sectional sofa covered most of the wall to his left, an oak coffee table, topped with more empty beer cans, sat cockeyed in front of it. The large fieldstone fireplace, which ran from the floor to the ceiling on the far wall, was filled with nothing but ashes. Gusts of cold air rushed down the chimney, blowing the ashes against the etched glass. Matching leather recliners, separated by a white tray table, sat on the edge of a large oval braided rug. All four windows had the drapes drawn tight. The air was dank and reeked of stale cigarette smoke.

Jimmy quietly and quickly stepped into the room, shuffling his feet along the hardwood floor. His head swiveled sharply toward the quivering light—toward the TV. He stepped further into the room, with Corey close on his heels. The television screen glowed in the semi–darkness of the room, casting eerie shadows on the wall. An old rerun of *Gilligan's Island*, the one where the telephone cable washes up on the shore of the lagoon, was on. The word *mute*, written in light blue letters on the bottom of the screen, blinked on and off.

The living room led to a long hallway, which led to three bedrooms towards the rear of the house. A single French door, with lace curtains draped across the panes of glass, divided the living room from the hallway.

Taggert and Corey pressed on, entering the hallway single file, guns leading the way. Jimmy was familiar with the layout of the house. Bobby's old bedroom was the first one on the left. He had spent many afternoons in his best friend's room stealing a peek at Ed's rather substantial collection of *Playboy* magazines. Bobby's sister's bedroom was directly across the way and his parent's room was at the end of the long corridor. Hallway walls were cluttered with knickknacks and family photos. An oversized grandfather's clock choked the hallway, its pendulum methodically swinging back and forth.

Sweat glistened off Mitchell Corey's forehead. A rush of adrenaline coursed through his veins, kicking his heart into overdrive. His breathing was rapid and shallow, churning out a steady stream of frosty smog. He felt cold and hot at the same time.

The first two bedrooms they passed were empty—nothing but beds, dressers, and closets full of old clothes and shoes. Neither bed was made. Sheets were crumpled up in piles and pillows were scattered. More beer cans and cigarette–filled coffee mugs littered dresser tops. The door to the third room, Ed and Nattie's bedroom, was closed. The hallway was narrow and didn't offer either man any cover. Jimmy stopped a foot and a half from the door and slowly reached for the doorknob. Corey crouched down and pointed his service revolver at the middle of the door. The elbow of his right hand rested on his thigh, his left hand steadied his gun.

"On three," Jimmy mouthed, holding up the first three fingers of his hand.

Corey gripped his pistol tighter and nodded. Small beads of sweat formed along his hairline, some ran down his face, streaking across his cheeks.

Jimmy carefully cracked the door and peered inside the room. A familiar, unwelcome, reddish brown stain caught his eye. *Dried blood*, he thought as he thrust the door open, sending it crashing hard into the wall. The stain was large, matted and thick—so thick that none of the green carpet showed through. A winding trail of blood led to the far side of the bed. Ed Ryan's double barrel shotgun lay abandoned on the floor, halfway between the door and bed. Jimmy followed the trail with his eyes, slowly turning his head, forcing himself to look. An overwhelming and incapacitating fear rose from the pit of his stomach. He swallowed hard and fought it back with all he had. A pair of well–worn, brown leather work boots jutted out from the end of the bed.

Jimmy knew instantly whom they belonged to.

Ed Ryan's lifeless body lay face up on the floor with both eyes opened wide. Rigor mortis had long settled in. His face was taut; muscles drew back his leathery skin, pulling his cracked lips past the gums, exposing yellowed teeth. Color was gone from his face, leaving the skin a ghastly whitish–blue hue. One arm was twisted across a blood–encrusted shirt, the other lay under the bed.

Jimmy hung his head and made the sign of the cross. Tears welled in his eyes. He bent over and gently closed Ed Ryan's eyes. "Say hello to Bobby for me," he whispered.

Corey checked the closet before joining the Sheriff.

"Max, come in," Jimmy said somberly, speaking into the walkie–talkie that was clipped to his shoulder.

"Gotcha, Sheriff. Go ahead," Max's voice crackled back a fraction of a second later.

"Ed Ryan's dead. The bastards murdered him. Tell Steve and Richie to head over here along with the M.E. Get a hold of Charlie Martin and have him get over here with one of his plows. The driveways filled with snow. Tell him I want everything plowed in towards the area to the left of the barn. I don't want any evidence that might be buried under the goddamn snow plowed onto the road. Agent Corey wants you to contact the FBI office in Buffalo and have them send a team of investigators."

"What about Nattie?" Max asked.

"No sign of her yet. We're going to check out the barn. We'll let you know—"

A dull scratching sound caught Jimmy's ear.

"Gotta go, Max. There's a noise coming from the basement," he whispered.

Mitchell Corey had already turned and was hurriedly walking back down the hall towards the basement. Jimmy was a step and a half behind him, still trying to shake the grisly image of Ed Ryan's corpse from his head. The entrance to the basement sat halfway between the foyer and kitchen. Its six–panel, solid oak door had a deadbolt and chain lock. Both of which were in the locked position. *Did I miss the noise when I passed by the door a couple of minutes ago? Could it be Nattie?* Jimmy wondered. His heart was racing again and his throat was dry—too dry to muster a spit. The faint scratching noise increased in frequency as the two men approached the basement, still, it was barely audible at best.

Jimmy turned the deadbolt and slid the chain off, letting it dangle freely. It swung back and forth, gently scraping the door.

"Nattie, is that you? It's me, Jimmy…Jimmy Taggert. I'm coming down."

There was a faint scratching noise again followed by what the Sheriff thought was a slight whimper. A glimmer of hope floated in the air. He crouched down and opened the door a crack, letting daylight seep into the dark, dank cellar. He saw something at the bottom of the stairs, something lying there, something moving—something still alive. He pushed the door open, letting more light cascade down the wooden steps.

At the bottom of the landing, against the darkness of the stone wall, a pair of eyes stared back.

The dark brown, boxy UPS truck's tires scraped against the curb as it rolled to a stop on Main Street. Worn brake pads screeched loudly against the drum. Danny Callahan jotted down a few quick notations in his black and white notebook before jumping down from the truck, and strolling into the Sheriff's office. A long rectangular package was tucked under his lanky arm. A portable CD player was clipped to his belt, headphones were snug to his ears. Springsteen's '*Born to Run,*' choked his eardrums and Danny Callahan was singing along—completely out of key and a beat and a half behind.

But he was belting it out as best he could. At $20.55 an hour, he didn't have a care in the world.

"Yo, Max. Got a package for the T–Man," he yelled as he swung the office doors open. "Needs your John Hancock on it."

"Be with you in a second, Danny," Max replied, covering the mouthpiece of the phone with the palm of his hand.

Danny lifted one side of the headphones off his ear, nodded, flashed a thumbs up sign and laid the box on a desk. "No probleeomo, dude," he said grinning. "I got all day. Take your time, Maximus. Hey, mind if I cop a doughnut?"

The basement steps creaked loudly under Jimmy's weight. He flipped the light switch on the wall and took a quick step down. "Son–of–a–bitch," he screamed, as he rushed down the remaining stairs.

The Ryans' yellow Labrador Retriever lay in a pool of blood on the landing. Its back was braced against the cold, stone wall. His fur was matted with dried blood. One end of an oversized chain was wrapped around a support post, the other around his neck. A large screwdriver was buried deep into his side, leaving none of its stainless steel shaft visible. His big brown eyes squinted from the light, the first he'd seen in close to a week. His breaths were shallow and weak. Whistling accompanied each painful exhale.

"It'll be okay, Cooper," Jimmy assured the dog as he gently stroked the its head. "Get me a bowl of water from the laundry room, will you?" he asked.

Corey returned a moment later and placed the bowl of fresh water on the landing. The dog was too weak to lift his head so Jimmy scooped the water and let him drink from his cupped hands.

"I'll check the rest of the basement while you take care of the dog," Corey said. He quickly moved through the basement without finding a sign of Nattie. Jimmy scooped up the dog and brought him upstairs, carefully laying him down on a small braided rug in the kitchen.

He clicked his walkie–talkie. "Max, it's me again. Come in."

"I'm here, boss. Go ahead."

"Get a hold of Richie and have him stop by the vets. Tell him to pick up Doc Adams on the way out here. They stabbed Cooper. He's alive, but barely. Tell him to bring blood with him…plenty of it."

"What the hell's wrong with them? That dog wouldn't hurt a fly. He's nothing but a big baby," Max answered angrily. "Anything on Nattie?"

"Nothing yet. We're heading to the barn now. I'll get back to you in a few minutes. Tell Richie to hurry. Cooper doesn't have too much time left."

"I'm on it, Chief."

* * *

Danny Callahan was well into his second doughnut by the time Max caught up with him. "Whatta ya got for me today, Danny?"

"Just one package. Special delivery. Sign here and she's all yours."

"Who's it from?"

"Don't know. There's no return address," Danny answered indifferently. He chomped down the last third of the peanut stick and swallowed it in one long gulp.

"Probably more flowers for the Sheriff. They've been coming in all week. His living room and office look like a floral shop."

Danny shook his head. "Negative on the flowers, Maximus. Don't know what it is but it ain't flowers. Too heavy for that—way too heavy, dude."

Max raised an eyebrow and gingerly took the package from Danny. "Everybody out of the building," he yelled. "Get out now!"

The barn stood tall and stark against the morning sky. Two hundred–year–old sycamores fenced it in on two sides. A thick coat of snow covered its tattered, bowed roof. Well–weathered cedar planks, splintering in spots, covered its sides. A copper weathervane was perched at the center of the roof. A solitary black bird sat atop it, barking out a warning. There wasn't a single window with intact glass, most were boarded up with plywood scraps. A squirrel ran along an overhead line that fed electricity to the barn. It stood on its hind legs, put its nose to the air and quickly scurried away as the two lawmen noisily plodded through the deep snowdrifts.

Jimmy slowly slid the barn door open, failing to notice the trip wire that ran from the far edge of the door to the Cadillac's ignition. Five packs of C–4 were strung together by a det cord that was wired to a spark plug. The bomb was crude but effective. As the door slid open it took up the wire's slack and tripped the engine, sending a spark to the plug—igniting the C–4 in the briefest of seconds.

The barn went up just as Richie and Steve arrived on the scene. Pieces of debris flew in every direction. Fire and smoke poured out huge holes in the walls and roof. Thick black smog quickly colored the sky. Windows in nearby houses were shattered to pieces. The force of the blast catapulted the two men high into the cold air. They looked like little more than rag dolls as their bodies crashed to the ground in a crumpled heap.

Darien County's part–time, one–man bomb squad was already at the Sheriff's Office when the bomb in the Ryans' barn lit up the sky. Sirens blared outside as first aid units and the fire department raced to the scene. An eerie feeling added to an already tense situation as the twenty–something bomb squad technician, Joe Hardaway, examined the mysterious package. He bent over the table, wearing his bulky outfit and clumsy gloves, and carefully sliced the wrapping paper, peeling it away a few excruciating millimeters at a time, exposing a plain white box. After painstakingly examining the box, he slowly lifted the cover up and off. An envelope, addressed to Sheriff Taggert, rested on top of a thick pile of tissue paper. Hardaway stepped back, lifted his blast visor up off his face, and handed the envelope to Max.

Max tore it open and removed a handwritten note.

Dear Sheriff Taggert:

I thought I'd lend a 'hand' to your investigation. Make sure you refrigerate it after opening. Thanks for your town's hospitality. Ed and Nattie were the perfect hosts. I just love 'em to death. You take care of yourself and look me up if you get a chance. I'll be waiting. Don't be a stranger.

Michael

Hardaway went back to work, carefully stripping away the tissue paper one sheet at a time. Max leaned forward, anxiously peering over his shoulder, concentrating more on the note than the package.

Hardaway gripped the last piece of tissue with his tweezers and slowly peeled it away. Suddenly, he screamed and jumped back, knocking Max to the floor. He ripped the blast shield from his face and gasped for air.

Max glanced at the contents of the box and quickly turned away, trying in vain to hold down his breakfast. Inside the box was Billy Joe Bouchard's decaying arm. One half of a set of handcuffs was attached to his withered wrist. Gaudy rings choked his stubby, bloated fingers. A nail was missing from his thumb and his skin was an ashen gray. The end of his arm, torn at the shoulder, was a mass of ruptured blood vessels and torn muscle tissue peeled back to the bone.

Max covered his nose and mouth with his sleeve, and slid the top back on the box.

CHAPTER 8

It's hard to imagine a more physically intimidating prison than Attica. It looks more like a medieval castle than a penitentiary. The prison sits on a hill off of Route 354 in the small town that gave rise to its infamous name. As you drive up the winding two–lane road you almost expect to find a moat encircling the mammoth structure, and the need for a drawbridge to enter its cavernous body. Its towering stone walls, twenty feet high and eight feet thick, are capped by an additional six feet of razor wire. A maze of infrared motion detectors, cameras, and photoelectric lights cover every square inch of the enormous complex that 2,100 inmates call home. Giant guard towers that rise twenty feet beyond the razor wire occupy its bulky corners. Each tower houses an arsenal of assault rifles, tear gas, and at least five sharpshooters, all with standing orders to shoot escapees on sight. Prisoners are locked down for 23 hours a day, seven days a week. Since its opening in 1931, there has never been a successful escape.

Jack Slater sat restless on the end of the cot in his darkened cell. Cockroaches crawled along damp and crumbling walls, staying in the safety of the shadows. A spider slowly spun an evening web, meticulously weaving its silky thread between metal bars. Several twisted sheets, strung together, were grasped firmly in the inmate's hand. He listened intently for the guard's solitary footsteps. It was a quarter to nine and the day's final count was just beginning.

Remember what Michael told you, he reminded himself. *You can do it. It's up to you.* He took long deep breaths…just like his stepbrother instructed. He was ready. He was focused. Slater's long blonde hair, tied back in a ponytail, lay flat against his green jumpsuit. He sported thick sideburns and a well–groomed goatee. His piercing deep blue eyes were cold and unforgiving. Muscular arms were dotted with tattoos and zigzagging scars.

The night guard, Johnny Hopper, dragged his keys along the metal handrail as he climbed the stairs to D block. The grating noise bothered him but he found comfort in the fact that it bothered the inmates even more. *He was in control and they needed reminding—constant reminding,* he thought. His size 10 steel–toed work boots echoed loudly on the metal grate steps. To add insult to injury, he whistled Lynard Skynard's '*Freebird*' as he calmly strolled up the stairs. "Time for bed, scumbags. Lights out, ladies," he mocked. His nasally voice was more irritating than the screeching of the keys on the handrail.

Slater's cell was the last one on the upper bay—exactly 84 steps from the top of the stairs to his cell. Eighty–four of Johnny Hopper's antagonizing steps. Hopper was still whistling *'Freebird'* as his boot hit the metal walkway for the thirtieth time. Slater took a deep breath, "It's show time," he whispered nervously. He sprung from the cot and tied one end of his sheet–rope to the top bar of his cell, ripping the persistent spider's work to shreds. He leaned forward, tilted an ear toward the walkway, and listened for a moment, silently counting another twenty steps before slipping a makeshift noose over his head and pulling it snug against his thick neck. He stepped on the edge of the cot and waited, taking long deep breaths, just like he'd been told to do.

"Sixty–eight…sixty–nine…seventy…seventy–one…seventy–two…seventy–three…seventy–four," Slater counted in a faint whisper. His skin was clammy and his throat was dry. His heart thumped loudly against his muscular chest. *It's now or never,* he thought, *too late to go back.* He took a deep breath and stepped off the edge of the cot just as Johnny Hopper's boot hit the floor for the seventy–seventh time. Just like he planned.

The noose tightened sharply, quickly cutting off the dangling inmate's air. His body convulsed and his legs flailed wildly, striking the cell door bars. Slater's eye's rolled back and he lost consciousness. *Just like his brother planned.*

"What the fuck," Hopper yelled as he approached Slater's cell. "We got a hanger," he screamed. "Crack open 24 D. Crack that fucker open. NOW!"

Hopper squeezed through the cell door as it slid slowly to the right. "You stupid prick. I'd let you die right here if it wasn't for the fucking paperwork. Next time kill yourself on someone else's shift," he grumbled as he cut Slater's limp body down.

Doctor Anthony Biondi held Slater's eyelid open with his stubby thumb and probed his eye with a penlight. "He'll live," Biondi announced after stuffing the penlight back into his lab coat. The doctor was short and stocky, a good sixty pounds overweight. A thick beard covered his burgeoning double chin. Whispers of gray streaked his dark hair. "Give him two aspirins and call me in the morning," he said, and winked. "He'd be dead if he swung for another twenty seconds or so. He's lucky you came by when you did."

Hopper sat at a nearby desk, leaning as far back as the chair would allow, looking as smug as usual. One leg rested on an opened drawer, the other on the desktop. His lanky arms were folded across his chest. "I guess I'm a hero, huh? And what do I get for it? Jack–shit, that's what. They should give me a bonus...cold hard cash...beaners...dead presidents...something I can use. The superintendent will probably give me a friggin' certificate. The only thing a certificate's good for is wiping your ass. Shit, I should have let Slater die. Save the state some money. The stupid bastard."

Dr. Biondi laughed. "You're a piece of work, Hopper. No doubt about it, humanitarian of the year, that's what you are," he said shaking his head. "I'll give him a shot of Valium. That should keep him sleeping through the night. I'll be by in the morning to check up on him."

"I'll be here in the morning, too, filling out a stack of paperwork, thanks to Slater. Sergeant wants it before noon, like anyone's gonna read it," Hopper complained. "If it were up to me I'd have him fill it out. See how he likes it. That is if the dumb–ass can even read or write."

Jack Slater opened his eyes no more than an eighth of inch, just far enough to steal a glimpse at his new surroundings before the nurse stuck a needle into his vein and flooded his body with a thoroughly soothing dose of Valium. *Fuck you, Hopper,* he thought as he drifted off. *I'll see you in the morning, pal. 'Freebird'* was cranking in his head.

Sheriff Taggert and Agent Corey had the good fortune of landing in a huge snowdrift that was curled around a tall stack of hay. Other than a few cuts, scrapes, and throbbing headaches, they were no worse for the wear. Deputies' Atwater and Thompson pulled them to their feet and helped brush the snow from their clothes. The barn fire roared out of control, heating the cold morning air. Burning debris floated down to the ground, sizzling as it hit the cold snow.

"I didn't see the trip wire until it was too late," Jimmy explained, half out of breath. "Their black Caddy's in there—or what's left of it. They must have had the C–4 wired to the plugs." He used his hat to clear the rest of the snow from his pants. "The Ryans' pickup's in there, too, but not the Impala. Have Max get an APB out on it. Have him check the bridges to Canada. I'm betting that they snuck across the border. It'll be a while before we'll be able to get into the barn and see if Nattie's in there. I hope to God she's not." The Sheriff fit his hat snugly to his head and turned toward Dr. Adams. "The dog's in the house, Doc. He's alive but in bad shape. I'd appreciate anything you can do for him."

Dr. Adams nodded, pulled his bag from Deputy Atwater's car, and rushed into the house.

"See if you can lend a hand. Would you, Steve?"

"You got it, Sheriff."

Michael Baker checked his watch and waited a moment before slowly backing the van out of the warehouse. He turned the police scanner on and leaned back, keeping the engine idling. "Just a few minutes longer, boys," he said calmly to Kyle Peterson and Danny Robinson. "The call should be coming in soon."

"What do you want to do with the drunk's body?" Robinson asked. He took a long drag from his cigarette and blew a ring of smoke into the crisp air. "Shouldn't we bury it or something? What if the police stop by?"

Peterson rolled down the window and spit a huge wad of brownish drool onto the ground. "I ain't burying nothing. My shoulder's still fucked–up." He lifted his arm over his head and winced. "See what I mean. I'm not going to be able to work out for a month as it is. Besides, there must be three feet of snow on the ground…maybe more. I say we leave him in the warehouse. I'm betting no one will even miss the poor bastard. He looked like a no good drunk to me. What do you think, boss?"

"We don't have time to mess with the body. They probably won't find him 'til spring. Nobody comes by here, especially in the winter.

He was unlucky enough to be in the wrong place at the wrong time. Hell, he shouldn't have been poking around here anyhow. Let's leave him for the rats. They'll eat most of him by the time the weather turns." Baker took off his sunglasses and cleaned the lenses with the end of his shirt. "You got rid of his wallet, didn't you?"

"Yeah, the cheap bastard didn't have any money though. All that was in it was a picture of his wife. She's one *ugly* lady, man. Ugly with a capital U...butt ugly! Hell, I'd have to put three bags over her face and *mine* before I thought about doin' her. Even then I'd need to be half in the bag. You could tie a bone around her neck and the dogs still wouldn't play with the bitch...that's how ugly she is," Peterson said laughing.

Baker laughed out loud and shook his head. "What was the stupid pricks name?"

"Holloway...I think," Peterson said, scratching his head. "Yeah, that's it. Cap Holloway," he replied.

Baker smiled. "I like the name. Sort of sounds like a movie star or something. Don't it?"

* * *

"Morning, Hopper," Doctor Biondi said as he passed by the disgruntled guard on his way to his office.

Hopper was hunched over a desk with a fistful of state forms in one hand and a couple of pencils in the other. "What the fuck's good about it, Doc? I should be home sleeping. Not here filling out these goddamn forms," he answered, not bothering to raise his head or wave.

Biondi smiled and shook his head but chose not to reply. He sat at his desk and went through his mail in the fifteen minutes he had before morning rounds.

Slater lay on the bed just outside his office door, pretending to sleep. He listened carefully as the doctor sliced through the envelopes one at a time. *Come on...come on...open it, motherfucker*, he said to himself.

There were two other inmates in the infirmary with Slater. Hector Gonzalez, was serving 25–to–life for murdering his wife and her lover with an ice pick. Franky, "The Worm" Morisano, was in for the full–ride, life without the possibility of parole. Seems "The Worm" shot and killed two of New York City's finest on St. Patrick's Day in '79 over a five dollar parking ticket. They caught up with him an hour later, sitting at a bar across the street, quietly eating lunch. Acting like he didn't have a care in the world.

Molly O'Brien, a full–figured nurse, in her early thirties, filled a tray with daily meds while a clerk made notes in a log. Her chestnut–brown hair lay gently on her shoulders. Hopper, the only guard on duty, was his usual irritating self. Sexual innuendoes flowed from his foul mouth at a rapid clip. Molly's occasional glares or sighs didn't phase him in the least. *She wants it,* he thought. *All of them want it!* He violated every inch of her body with his probing eyes, he longed for a glimpse of cleavage as she bent forward in a white dress that clung tightly to her ample mounds. *Give it to me, baby. Show me what you've got, bitch.* Demented thought after demented thought surged from his pubescent brain.

Biondi picked up a thin white envelope, without a return address, and slit it open without giving it a second thought. He unfolded the neatly creased letter written on buff–colored paper and immediately dropped it on the desk after reading the eleven words printed in Arial type on the page. "Son–of–a–bitch," he moaned.

You have just been exposed to Anthrax.
Have a nice day!

"Hopper," Biondi yelled.

Hopper didn't respond.

"Hopper," the doctor screamed again, in a booming voice.

The guard reluctantly pulled his attention away from Molly's dress and slowly turned his head. "Yeah, whatta ya want?" he snarled.

"Lock the doors. Don't let anyone in or out. We've got an Anthrax threat. You call security while I dial 911. It's probably a hoax, but we can't take any chances. Kill the air–conditioning and close the vents."

"You've got to be fucking kidding. Tell me it's a goddamn practical joke, Doc. Don't do this to me. I've got plans for this afternoon. BIG GODDAMN PLANS!"

"It's no joke. Looks like none of us are going anywhere soon. At least not until the Hazmat team gets here and decontaminates everything…us included."

* * *

"That's it, gentlemen. Right on schedule. It's show time," Michael Baker announced just after Dr. Biondi's 911 call came in over the scanner. "Kick the tires and light the fire." He backed the large white van out of the snow–covered access road, turned onto Route 354, and hit the siren and lights. "Both of you get dressed, we'll be there in under ten minutes. Make sure you grab the briefcase, Kyle."

Peterson lifted the steel briefcase up and laid it in his lap. "Got it right here," he said. Robinson slid a fresh clip into his AK–47 and quickly got dressed.

* * *

Baker, Peterson, and Robinson strolled confidently into Attica's medical unit wearing Hazmat Level A protective gear from head to toe. Tinted visors conveniently shielded their faces.

"You guys sure got here fast," Dr. Biondi commented, glancing at his watch. "I just called it in a few minutes ago."

"It's your lucky day, Doc. We were on a training mission just down the road a bit when the call came across the radio. All dressed up with nowhere to go—if you know what I mean," Baker replied. His eyes drifted across the room to Jack Slater.

"How long's this gonna take?" Hopper growled, pushing his way past Biondi.

"Shouldn't take too long, Officer. It's probably a hoax. We've had three similar calls this week and all of them turned out to be false alarms. But we've got to be sure. Got to go by the book. Rather be safe than sorry, right? We're going to have to decontaminate the entire area, including each of you."

"Are you out of your fucking mind? That will take all afternoon. I've got plans. It's a friggin' joke. The letter's bogus. So why don't you and the rest of your Star Trek crew contact Scottie and get your asses beamed back to the Enterprise or wherever the hell you came from!"

Baker grabbed hold of Hopper's arm and squeezed tightly. "You're going to sit your ass down, call security and tell them that everything's under control."

Hopper yanked his arm away and stepped back. "Listen, Captain James T. Jerkoff, or whatever the hell your name is. Who died and left you in charge? Touch me again and I'll cuff your ass. Right after I kick the shit out of you and the rest of your ghost busting faggots."

Baker slid his hand into a backpack and pulled out his 9mm pistol. "Sit your skinny ass down and dial the phone, motherfucker. Do it or I'll splatter your brains, what little there are, all over the fat doctor's bright white lab coat." He jammed the pistol up against Hopper's forehead. "It's your call, shit–for–brains."

Peterson and Robinson pulled out assault rifles and pushed the others against the wall.

Sweat rolled off Hopper's balding forehead, splattering his shirt. A steady stream of warm urine ran down his leg, dripping on his leather boots and ponding on the floor. He swallowed hard and nodded sheepishly. I'll…I'll ca…ca…call right no…now," he stammered.

"Good. You're not as stupid as you look," Baker cracked. He turned toward Peterson. "Unstrap Jack and give him your suit. The rest of you head to the back room with my associate, Mr. Robinson. He has a rather short fuse so I'd advise each of you to do exactly as he asks. He has several pieces of rope and duct tape for your bondage pleasure. No harm will come to you if you play by the rules…my rules." He turned his attention back to the guard again. "I believe you have a phone call to make, Officer Hopper. Dial the phone and say only what I tell you to say." Baker clamped Hopper's jaw with his hand and squeezed. "Do you understand?"

Hopper nodded.

"Excellent. Now tell your friends that everything's fine, that it was a false alarm and that we'll be coming out shortly."

Jack Slater pulled the rope tight to Hopper's wrist, cutting off his circulation. "How's that feel, hack? A little too tight?" He leaned forward and stared into the terrified guard's eyes. Enjoying the moment. Enjoying the power. "Awful quiet now, aren't we, Johnny?"

"I saved your life yesterday. You'd be dead if it wasn't for me. Let me go. Please let me go," Hopper pleaded.

Slater took a scalpel from the table and slowly rotated it between his fingers. "You don't mind if I borrow this for a minute or two, do you, Doc?"

Hopper followed the scalpel's movement with his eyes. Sweat poured from his trembling body, soaking his shirt and hair. His pants reeked of urine. "I'll get you out of here. I can do it. I'll get you past the gates. No one will know. I promise, Jack. You need me. Don't do this. I've got a wife and kids at home. Please for the love of God, don't hurt me."

Slater stared at Hopper for a long, agonizing moment and smiled. He tore a piece of duct tape from the roll and covered the guard's mouth. "How much time you figure we got, Michael?"

"Fifteen minutes. Give or take a few. Enough to finish what you started, little brother."

Biondi sat in the chair next to Hopper. Molly and the clerk were directly across from him. Gonzalez and Morisano were shackled to chairs in Exam Room Two.

Baker took the metal briefcase from Peterson and laid it on Biondi's desk. Florescent lights reflected off its smooth shiny surface. Twenty–four individually wrapped, two–pound blocks of a reddish–brown clay–like substance were tightly packed into the leather–lined briefcase. A digital timer, wired to an electronic detonator, was sandwiched between the two–pound blocks.

Slater cut deeply into Hopper's face, starting at his jaw and slowly working his way across his ruddy cheek. Blood squirted out onto the guard's dull gray uniform, quickly coloring it red. Hopper's muffled screams fell on deaf ears as his body shuddered. Unrelenting pain burned through his body. The wooden chair he was bound tightly to creaked loudly as he struggled to free himself. He desperately tried pulling away but Slater had a fistful of hair, holding his head firmly in place. His protruding eyes followed the path of the scalpel. Its razor sharp blade easily sliced through his soft flesh, leaving a stream of warm blood in its wake. Molly O'Brien and Dr. Biondi looked on in absolute horror. The color quickly drained from the clerk's face, leaving it a ghostly shade of white.

Slater's lips curled into a haunting smile. His deep blue eyes were cold and piercing, his hand, steady and strong. He started humming '*Freebird*' as he guided the scalpel further up Hopper's quivering face. "It's sort of like carving a turkey," he said laughing.

Michael Baker glanced over his shoulder, admiring his brother's work, before turning his full attention to the metal briefcase. Robinson stood guard over the other hostages, concentrating more on Molly O'Brien's tight dress and ample cleavage than Slater's handiwork, devouring her with dark, hungry eyes. He wet his lips with his tongue and rubbed the stubble on his chin with his hand. Peterson squatted by the door and kept a silent watch.

Deputy Atwater poked his head out of the squad car. "Hey, Sheriff, I know you've got more important things on your mind, but old lady Holloway's called the station twice since you left. Seems old Cap didn't come home again last night, like that's never happened before," he joked. "She thinks he ran into some trouble. 'Cording to her, he was heading towards Prospect Point. Said he muttered something about fetching some scrap wood to fix the chicken coop. Anyhow, the old lady's driving me crazy. She's looking for us to issue an APB. Said she's got a bad feeling. Mumbled some crap about woman's intuition. What ya want me to tell the old gas–bag?"

"Woman's intuition my ass. If she had even once ounce of intuition she wouldn't have married the bum. Hell, I bet he's holed up somewhere nursing a fifth of Jack, trying hard to erase memories of her constant nagging from what's left of his brain. She knows damn well that he goes off on a wicked bender every few months." Jimmy laughed, "hell, he ain't fixin' the chicken coop…he's flown it. Can't say I blame him neither. She'd drive me to drink, all right. Christ, that woman can yap with the best of 'em. Tell her that'll he'll probably come crawling home tonight and if he's not we'll send a car up to the old warehouse at Prospect Point to check it out. Anything else going on?"

"Only another anthrax threat. Third one this week," Deputy Atwater reported.

Jimmy shook his head. "Where's this one?" he asked, stepping closer to the barn.

"Attica."

Agent Corey turned sharply. "Attica Prison?" he asked.

"Yeah, it's about 10 miles east of here. Why?" Atwater replied.

"Baker's stepbrother is incarcerated there."

"I don't believe in coincidences. Do you, Corey?" Jimmy asked.

"No, Sheriff, I never have. Do you have enough gas in your truck to get us to the prison?"

"More than enough. Let's roll."

CHAPTER 9

Hopper's eyeball dangled for a split–second, held by fraying threads of tendon and muscle, before detaching completely and falling to the floor by his feet. He let out a faint guttural moan, slumped forward, and quickly lost consciousness.

"Looks like we've got one less eyewitness," Slater jeered. "Yep, guess we don't quite see eye–to–eye anymore, huh?"

Baker closed the briefcase and carefully slid it under Biondi's desk. "Perfect timing, Jack. We're ready to go. Get into Kyle's spacesuit, we're bustin' out."

Jimmy's truck slid wildly on the snow–covered road as he hastily made his way east on Route 354.

"We're just about halfway there. We'd be there by now, if it weren't for this damn snow," Jimmy grumbled. "You think Baker's there? Think he's at Attica?"

"It's his style. Fits his profile. He'd break Slater out more for the notoriety than for his brother's sake. Attica's never had a successful escape. That's awful enticing to a guy like Baker. He loves the publicity. Loves to read about himself. Can't get enough of it." The truck slid under an old railroad bridge and continued along the winding road. "He did a bank job in Cleveland last year. We were a couple of steps behind him, as usual. We located his hideout a few hours after the prick bolted. He'd only been there for a day and a half, but managed to buy four different newspapers. He even had the morning and afternoon editions of the same paper. Baker cut out all of the articles having to do with the bank job. The conceited bastard probably keeps them in a scrapbook. Yeah he loves the attention. Our shrink department profiled him. Says he's looking for the attention he missed as a kid…displaced parental attention disorder, so they say," the FBI agent said shaking his head.

"You buy that?" Jimmy asked warily. He glanced up at a flock of blackbirds flying high overhead before turning his attention back to the road.

"Hell, I don't know. It's part of the reason, I suppose. Personally, I think he's a fucking psychopath and like all good psychopaths…he loves his work. The problem with Baker is that the bastard's smart. Too damn smart. We haven't been able to get a bead on him. He's always changing his appearance and his MO, and his jobs are extremely well planned. He always leaves himself an out, never paints himself into a corner. He'll hit a bank, disappear for six months, hit another, and disappear again. He's methodical and patient. More patient than you'd expect. We know he has a hideout somewhere deep in the woods in Canada, but haven't had any luck finding it. To make matters worse, he and Peterson are outdoor survival experts, and they're heavily tied into underground networks. Mostly radical militia groups. They can stay underground for a long time. A *very* long time."

Jimmy rolled down the window and spit. Cold air rushed into the car, swirling through the cab. "I don't care how smart he is. Sooner or later everyone makes a mistake and we'll be there when he does. I swear I'll be there, and Michael Baker will regret the day he set foot in Darien."

"Who knows, maybe today's the day. Maybe he's going down today," Corey replied half–heartily.

Jimmy scratched his chin. "Baker doesn't strike me as a bank robber. It's not glamorous enough for his ego. What's his end game? Why steal the explosives from the military base? What do you suppose he's planning?"

"That would be the $64,000 question. We think Baker's doing the five and dime stuff to finance something bigger…much bigger. Something that's more in line with his expansive ego."

"Any ideas?"

"Nothing. I don't have a clue, but I've got a feeling that's been gnawing at my gut. It's been eating at me day and night. Hell, I must go through a bottle of Tums every week. He's planning on making a statement, and whatever he's planning is going to be big. It'll make Oklahoma City look like a walk in the park, and the Unabomber look like some high school punk setting off pipe bombs behind his old man's barn."

"Domestic terrorism?"

"Yeah. *Generation X* is extremely bad stuff. It's something we wish we could dis–invent. You could stuff five hundred pounds of it into the back seat of a compact car and still have room for the family dog. Five hundred pounds would easily level two city blocks, maybe more. I can't begin to imagine what a van full of it would do. We have no way of detecting it. It was designed for covert operations. It's practically invisible. Christ! Dogs can't even smell it."

"What's his cause? Who's the son–of–a–bitch hate?"

"Baker's not your run–of–the–mill anti–government zealot. He doesn't hate Jews, blacks or gays. Personally, I don't think he's motivated by hate."

Jimmy rolled his window up, "then what motivates him?"

"Fame and money. He'll kill if he has to and he'll kill to make a point, but I don't think it's what drives him. Don't get me wrong, he doesn't have a problem pulling the trigger. He's a true sociopath. No mercy. No remorse. No second chances. You throw in the fact that he's a genius, a perfectionist, and has to be the very best at whatever he does, and you get one scary human being. You get Michael Baker."

The white van drove slowly through the main gates at Attica and turned west on Route 354. Dark clouds pushed away the late–morning sun, enveloping the valley in an eerie darkness. Peterson was behind the wheel; a wad of chewing tobacco was stuffed in his cheek. Danny Robinson was riding shotgun. Baker and Slater were in the back of the van.

"Hell, that was easier than I thought it was going to be," Baker boasted, as he and his brother slid out of their Hazmat suits.

"Yeah, those stupid hacks thought I was one of them. You were right about the uniform. They bought it lock, stock, and barrel," Peterson snickered. He spit into a mug and wiped brown drool from his chin.

Jack Slater leaned forward into the cab. "Well, do me a favor and get rid of it when we stop. I don't want to see another fucking hack uniform as long as I live. Anytime I see someone in it, I want to kick the shit out of 'em."

Peterson grinned, "I'll take it off and burn it for you, Jack," he replied.

Slater nodded, leaned back, and turned toward his brother. "So where we headed?"

"Across the border. It'll be too hot around here. We'll lay low for while until the dust settles a bit. We've got one more job to pull before the real deal."

Slater slipped a sweatshirt over his head and tucked a pistol into his pants. "What about the suitcase?"

"Shit, I almost forgot," Baker said, pulling a small black transmitter from his pocket and handing it to his brother. "Would you care to do the honors?"

Slater grinned and pressed the small red button. "I wish I could see the look on Hopper's face."

Jimmy pointed to his left. "The prison's just over the next hill. We should see the guard towers any second—"

A thundering explosion rocked the ground, followed by a tall billowing plume of fire and smoke.

"What the hell is that?" Taggert yelled.

Corey rolled down his window and stuck his head out into the crisp air. "Attica would be my first guess. Looks like our boy is there." He tucked his head back in the truck and turned toward Jimmy. "Does this puppy have much more under the hood?"

Jimmy shifted the truck into fourth and punched the accelerator. "Do me a favor and load the shotgun that's behind your seat. Then tear the top off the box of shells and dump them into my coat pocket, will you?"

As they cleared the crest of the hill they could see the damage. C building was completely obliterated, transformed into a heap of stone and twisted steel. Smoke rose high into the air, engulfing three of the guard towers in a thick black fog. Smaller explosions occurred randomly, igniting fires and keeping rescuers a safe distance from the ruins.

"*Generation X?*" Taggert asked.

Corey nodded. "Believe it or not, looking at the damage, he didn't use all that much. It could have been worse. He could have leveled the place."

Jimmy looked at Corey. "He's saving it," he said.

"That's what scares me. Saving it for *what*?"

⁂

Baker rushed to the back of the van and stared out the window. "Holy shit! Look at that, will you? Christ, that's a beautiful site. Ain't it, boys!"

Slater stood next to his brother and marveled at the devastation. "Son–of–a–bitch, Michael. What the hell did you use? It looks like we nuked the place."

"We've got a pickup truck at 12 o'clock," Peterson announced. "Stay out of sight, Jack."

Robinson slipped the safety off and gripped his rifle with sweaty palms. Baker couldn't pull himself away from the inferno. The flickering glow of fire reflected in his dark eyes.

⁂

Jimmy turned towards Corey. "Don't ya think it's a little odd that the white van up ahead didn't pull over to look at the fire? It's not everyday that you see a prison going up in smoke."

"You read my mind. The driver seems to be in a hurry. Wouldn't you say?"

"How ya coming with the shotgun?"

Corey fed the last shell into the chamber and pumped it once. "She's ready to go."

Jimmy nodded, slid his pistol from its holster, and laid it in his lap. "Maybe today's the day we're not a step behind Baker. Maybe today's the day that bastard goes down."

⁂

"It's Peterson," Jimmy yelled as his pickup quickly rushed past the van. A swatch of road spray crashed against his windshield and his truck started to fishtail.

Peterson's eyes grew wide. "It's the fucking Sheriff," he yelled, stepping on the gas.

Baker watched as Jimmy righted the truck and turned around. "He's made us. Step on it, Kyle."

"Taggert's a better cop than I gave him credit for. Either that, or he's got one hell of a horseshoe stuck up his ass. Hmm, let's see who's riding shotgun," Baker said, raising a pair of binoculars to his face and adjusting the sights "You know, I believe that's Mitchell Corey sitting next to the Sheriff. Surprise...surprise...surprise."

"Who the hell is Mitchell Corey?" Robinson asked nervously.

"An FBI agent that's been on my ass for years. We're not going to be able to outrun them. Not in this pig. Looks like we go to plan B. Give me a minute, and then pull over, Kyle."

Slater stood and grabbed his brother by the arm, squeezing it tightly. "What the fuck are you talking about? We're not pulling over. Not with all this firepower. Not without a fight. I ain't going back to prison. I'll die before I go back to the hole."

"Do you know how many pounds of explosives are in this van? All it'll take is one fucking shot to light us up. You won't even have time to bend over and kiss your ass goodbye. You're not going back to prison. No one is. Relax, I've got a backup plan. You know I've always got one. Trust me." Baker pulled opened a door to a large storage cabinet on the side of the van. "I've got our insurance policy right here."

"What the hell's going on? They're pulling over," Corey said.

"I don't like this. I don't like it at all." Jimmy swung his pickup across the road and both men got out, using the truck for cover.

The back door of the van opened after a brief moment and Baker calmly stepped out onto the snow–covered road. "Good afternoon, gentlemen," he said, walking towards them. He was wearing a wool hunter green sweater with leather patches at the elbows and shoulders. His whitewashed jeans were tucked neatly into a pair of Cougar hiking boots and an M.I.T. baseball cap was fit snug to his head. Dark sunglasses covered his piercing blue eyes. "You look as though you've put on a little weight, Mitchell. I thought you'd drop a few pounds after chasing my ass all over the country. A few too many doughnuts, I'd guess." He smiled and turned toward the Sheriff. "And Jimmy, those bags under your eyes look awful. Aren't you getting enough sleep? Hell, you have the whole bed to yourself, or are you shacking up with some pretty young *thang* already, you sly old–dog?" His smile turned into a broad grin. "I must admit that I'm a tad bit surprised to see the two of you. I thought—"

"PUT YOUR HANDS ON YOUR HEAD AND DROP TO YOUR KNEES. DO IT NOW OR I'LL DROP YOU! AS SURE AS YOU'RE STANDING THERE I"LL KILL YOU!" Taggert yelled.

Baker smiled and took another step forward. "I believe you're under the illusion that *you're* in control, Sheriff. Let's review what happened the last time you thought that *you* were in control. Shall we?" Baker stood in the middle of the road with his hands folded across his chest. "Poor Mark Coleman's in a wheelchair for life. He can kiss that baseball scholarship goodbye, and his grades aren't even good enough to get him into retard U. He'll probably end up drinking his disability checks away in a rooming house full of drunks and prostitutes, and wallowing in self–pity the rest of his pathetic life. So it looks like his life's pretty much in the crapper…over before it started, as they say. Then there's Joe Morgan. The poor bastard didn't have life insurance so the wife and six kids he couldn't support when he was alive are pretty much in the shitter, too. His old lady will end up working two jobs. Won't be home for the rug–rats. At least not when it counts. They'll start doing drugs, stealing, maybe a couple of daddy's little angels will get knocked–up while their brothers spend time in the county jail. They'll all be collecting welfare checks one way or another, and poor Joe Morgan will be rolling over in his grave.

Then, there's the lovely Mrs. Anne Taggert, just days from retirement and living happily ever after. Boy, I bet that eats you up inside. Tears you apart...doesn't it? I bet that's what gives you those bags under your eyes. And let's not forget Ed Ryan, that social security guzzling motherfucker. Hell, you should thank me for greasing the old geezer. The goddamn social security system's going to hell in a hand basket because these old fucks don't know when to die. All this talk about trying to save social security. Hell, it doesn't take a genius. Kill the old people. End of *fucking* problem. Killing the old man was a freebie. I saved the government some money. Should get a reward or something. Don't you think?" Baker looked at Taggert and sneered. "You know what all of them had in common, Sheriff?"

"You son–of–a–bitch!" Jimmy shouted, rising to his feet.

Corey reached up and pulled him hard to the ground. "Don't let him get to you. He wants you to lose control. He wants you to act emotionally." He squeezed Jimmy's arm forcefully, enough to cut off the flow of blood. "Get a hold of yourself."

Baker laughed. "Every one of them died because *you* thought *you* were in control that day. Didn't you? All you had to do was sit back and let us leave instead of playing super cop. Hell, the money was insured. No one was going to lose a dime."

Jimmy tightened the grip on his pistol and cocked the hammer. "I'm not going to ask you again. Put your hands on top of your head and get down on your knees. Tell your friends to throw out their guns and come out of the van one at a time. Do it or I'll *grease* you."

Baker raised his arms high into the air. "Hey, I'm not armed. You wouldn't shoot an unarmed man. Would you? I've never studied criminal law, but I do believe that would be against the penal code in most states. At least that's what all the TV lawyers say. Besides, I'm willing to give you a second chance. A second chance to make the right decision. Most people don't get two chances, but I'm a forgiving kind of a guy. Truth is, I've got a soft spot in my heart for you,

Jimmy. You kinda remind me of my old man." Baker turned and snapped his fingers.

Kyle Peterson emerged from the van holding Nattie Ryan tight to his body. A pistol was pointed at her head. Nattie looked pale and weak, but otherwise unharmed.

"It's your call. We can do this the hard way, or the easy way. All you have to do is throw me the keys to your truck, let us leave, and no one else gets hurt. We'll get out of Dodge, Sheriff…won't ever come back, either. You do that and I'll let Nattie live. If you don't, then you'll have her blood on your hands. And you would have been responsible for three of the Ryans' deaths. Yeah, I heard all about poor Bobby Ryan. How he took *your* turn on point. How he saved *your* life. Bobby and the old man are dead because of you. Can you live with being responsible for the old lady's death as well? Shit, if I were the other Ryan kids, I'd stay as far away from you as possible. With friends like you, who needs enemies?"

"Don't listen to him, Jimmy. He killed those people…not you. He'll kill her no matter what you do. Don't let him get away. Think of how many more people will die if he walks. I've got a shot. Let me take it. Let's end this here and now," Corey pleaded. "We may never get another chance."

Jimmy's heart raced, hammering against his chest. Puffs of warm air billowed from his lungs, evaporating into the wintry air. A paralyzing fear rose from the pit of his stomach, choking his thoughts. He looked into Nattie's eyes—into the sadness and pain. He gripped his pistol tighter and steadied his arm against the hood of the truck. His palms were covered in a thick, cold sweat.

"Time's a–wasting. You've got thirty seconds," Baker warned. "Killing doesn't mean a thing to me. It's as easy as deciding what socks to wear in the morning. I won't have problem sleeping either way. How will *you* sleep tonight if Nattie dies?"

"I'll take Peterson. You take out Baker," Corey whispered. "Take the shot. Take the shot while you can, damn it! It's now or never!"

Jimmy looked at Baker, glanced at Corey, and turned to Baker again. He closed his eyes and took a deep breath. "Let her go. Let her go and you're free to leave," he yelled.

"It doesn't work that way, Jimmy. You throw your keys and weapons over here and I'll release her. You have my word on it."

"Your word's good for shit!"

"Maybe so, but shit's all you've got and beggars can't be choosy. Fifteen seconds, Jimmy. What's it going to be?"

Peterson cocked the hammer on his pistol and pressed it firmly against Nattie's head, pushing her thin gray hair to the side. He leaned forward, drew a wad of slobber and chew from his cheek and spit it on the road next to his boot.

"We'll throw the keys if you release her. The guns will come as soon as she's ten feet away from you."

Baker took the hat off his head and ran his fingers through his short hair. "Fair enough, Sheriff. Toss the keys to me and Nattie walks. But if she puts her foot down at the eleven–foot mark and your guns aren't on the ground at my feet I'll have the boys tear her open with more rounds than you can imagine. There won't be enough left of her to fill a can of sardines."

"Don't do it. For Christ sake don't—" Corey's plea fell on deaf ears.

Jimmy flung the keys high into the air, landing at Baker's feet. "Let her walk."

Baker slid his cap back on, turned to Peterson, and nodded. A smug smile made it's way to his face.

Nattie stumbled forward. Her long bony fingers held her tattered wool coat tight to her body. Strong gusts of cold wind whipped her face, brushing her hair back. Her steps were slow and shaky. Her ashen face showed all of her eighty–two years. She looked old and frail—more frail than Jimmy could ever remember.

Baker silently counted as Nattie feebly placed her foot on the cold snow for the tenth time. “Stop right there. Don’t take another step, grandma. Not until Sheriff Taggert keeps up his end of the deal.”

Corey turned toward Jimmy. “This is a mistake. You can’t trust him,” he whispered.

“I’ve got no choice. Nattie’s been like a mother to me. I can’t take any chances. Not with her. Enough people have died already.”

“Quit your jabbering, ladies, and toss those heaters over here. All of ‘em. Come on, a deal’s a deal.”

Jimmy looked at Corey. “You’ve got to trust me on this one. It ain’t over ‘til it’s over. Hand over the shotgun and your revolver.”

Mrs. Ryan stood shivering in the middle of the road. Peterson kept his pistol trained on her while Slater and Robinson crouched down in the van, each nervously clutching an assault rifle. “I’m not going back to prison. No way am I going back there again,” Slater murmured.

Beads of sweat rolled down Robinson’s face. “This is taking too long. I don’t like it. I don’t like it one bit,” he grumbled.

Jimmy slowly rose to his feet.

“Smart move, Sheriff. Now all you’ve got to do is toss them over here. Toss them here and the old–lady lives.”

The two pistols and shotgun landed in the snow bank a few feet to Baker’s left.

“I kept my end of the bargain. Now keep yours. Let her go.”

Baker bent down and collected the keys and weapons. “I just have one more request.”

“What is it?” Jimmy asked angrily.

“Tear the microphone out of your truck and pitch it over here. I can’t have you calling for back up, now can I?”

Jimmy reached through the window of the truck, ripped the microphone from the radio, and flung it across the road. “Let her go.”

Baker crushed the microphone with his boot and smiled. "I'm a man of my word. You can join them, Mrs. Ryan. You're free to go."

Nattie was a few short steps away from the safety of the truck when Baker nonchalantly raised the shotgun and squeezed the trigger. Two shotgun blasts shattered the serenity of the valley. She hit the snow–covered ground with a muffled thud a split second later.

CHAPTER 10

Jimmy's truck tires exploded, rubber flew off its rusty rims, and air escaped in a loud whoosh. Baker lowered the shotgun and grinned. "That's in case you have a spare set of keys, Constable," he said, and winked. "Well, it's been entertaining gentlemen, but I really must be going." He turned and calmly strolled back to the van, leaving behind a loud bellowing laugh in his wake. Peterson kept his pistol trained on the two men as he cautiously backed up one step at a time.

Jimmy rushed to Nattie's aid as Peterson swung the rear doors closed and the van quickly sped away. Baker stood in the back of the van, staring out the window. Huge plumes of thick black smoke, from the rubble of the prison, rose high into the sky, choking what little sunlight seeped through the dark, haunting clouds. Emergency sirens pierced the damp morning air, drowning out the blackbirds' calls. He watched, with an apathetic look on his face as Jimmy pulled Nattie to her feet and Corey draped a blanket over her bony shoulders.

"I want you to wait in the truck, Nattie. You'll be safe there, someone will be along shortly," the sheriff said quietly as he helped her step into the comfort of the cab. "There's a thermos full of soup in the glove compartment. It's nothin' close to your home cooking but it's hot and gets the job done. I want you to eat as much of it as you can. You need to get your strength back. Okay?"

Nattie offered a faint smile. "I'll be fine, Jimmy. I look worse than I feel."

Jimmy gently tucked the blanket under her legs and kissed her forehead. "I'll be back. I promise." Before he could back out of the truck he felt Nattie's arthritic hand grab hold of his collar and pull him close. He felt the warmth of her breath on his wind–chapped face.

"Jimmy?" she whispered.

"Yes, Nattie. What is it?"

She pulled on his collar until his ear was less than an inch from her blistered lips. "Don't let them get away. They killed Ed. Shot him like a dog." Tears welled in her eyes and her voice trembled. "He was a good man, a peaceful man. Wouldn't hurt a fly. He didn't deserve to die like that…no one does. Chase 'em through hell and back if you have to. Just like you did with the bastards that killed Bobby. Don't let them get away." She raised a clenched fist in the air. Her eyes narrowed and darkened. "There's a reckoning that needs to happen, Jimmy. Just like it says in the Bible…an eye for an eye."

Jimmy saw a deep, penetrating coldness in her eyes that he'd never seen before. "Yes, ma'am, an eye for an eye. Nothing less," he said backing out of the cab.

Corey looked around and shrugged his shoulders. "Umm…I hate to burst your bubble, but we don't have any wheels and I don't think we'll catch them on foot. Not unless you're a *whole* lot faster than you look."

Jimmy smiled and motioned Corey to the back of the truck. "We don't exactly need wheels out here. Give me a hand with this will you?" he asked, peeling the black tarp back off the bed of the truck.

"I'll be damned! You sly son–of–a–gun…a goddamn snowmobile."

"Oh, this is more than a just a goddamn snowmobile. It's a '98 Yamaha SRX 700. It's got, 696 cubic centimeters of displacement under the hood, triple cylinders, liquid cooling, a digital ignition, fuel injection, and a bore stroke ratio that rocks!"

Corey shook his head. "I'm not what you would call *machine* literate. Hell, I have trouble starting my lawnmower. What does all that gobbledygook mean for those of us who happen to be mechanically challenged?"

"It's fast! Really friggin' fast! Zero to sixty in under ten seconds, and 95 miles per hour on straight–aways. It's the fastest commercial snowmobile on the planet. Of course, I've made a few modifications and believe me…it screams! Come on, grab a ramp and ease her down."

Corey smiled. "In lay terms…it's got balls."

"You got that right!"

"That's all you had to say," Corey joked. He slid the metal ramp into place at the end of the tailgate and pulled on the snowmobile. "What are we going to do if we catch them? We can't exactly run them off the road with this sucker. Not unless it's got some other features you haven't mentioned."

"I've got a shotgun mounted on the right side and a Beretta stowed under the seat. All you need to do is load the shotgun with the shells you dumped in my coat pocket and I'll handle the pistol. Baker's only got one way out of the valley. Route 354 curls around an abandoned salt mine. We're going to take a short cut across old–man Hinkle's farm. We'll shave almost two miles off the trip and with a bit of luck…come out a few klicks ahead of the pricks."

"An ambush, huh?"

"Yep. A good old–fashioned ambush. Shoot first and ask questions later. Come on, let's get this bad boy on the road."

Baker held up Jimmy's pistol and laughed. "Ah, there's nothing quite like a cop's gun. Now is there? We played Taggert for the chump he is."

Peterson glanced at him and offered a faint smile.

"What's the matter, man?"

"I'll be glad when we're out of here. We've been here too long," he said, still clutching his pistol tightly while staring out the window. His eyes darted nervously back and forth across the road.

Baker leaned forward and patted him on the back. "Don't worry, partner. It's a nonstop express from here on out. We'll ditch the van and head across the border just like we planned. We'll be drinking Canadian beer in an hour…maybe less. First two rounds are on me."

Peterson nodded without saying a word. He continued to stare blankly out the window. The sound of wet snow scraping against the floorboards created a constant hum in the back of the van, muffling the annoying bickering between Robinson and Slater as they argued over which radio station to listen to.

Baker pulled up a wooden crate and sat down next to Peterson. "What's on your mind? What's bothering you?"

"I don't know. But I've got a bad feeling. Just like I did on that job in Kansas City when we ran into two off–duty cops cashing their paychecks. Remember? Christ, we were lucky to get out of there alive. Something don't feel right. Taggert gave in too quickly. Guys like him don't give up. Hell, we killed his friggin' wife." Peterson shook his head. His eyes closed to a squint. "I don't know. Maybe it's nothing. Maybe I'm just tired."

"Taggert didn't have a play. We backed him into a corner. I knew he wouldn't let the old lady get greased. He and Corey are sitting back there with their thumbs up their ass," Baker said laughing. He handed Taggert's pistol to Peterson. "Here, take his gun. It's nothing sexy…just your standard police issue, but the price was right."

Peterson took the gun and stuffed it into his pocket without looking up. The sky darkened and a light drizzle began to fall.

Jimmy pulled the throttle back and opened it up full. The snowmobile screamed across the virgin snow that blanketed Hinkle's barren cornfields, throwing a thick cloud of snow and mist in its wake. Wind raked his face, leaving it cold and numb. Corey wrapped his long arms around the sheriff's waist, squeezing tightly. He buried his face in the middle of Jimmy's back, shielding it from the cold.

The last mining cart full of rock salt had been scraped from tunnels deep within the Prospect Point Salt Mine more than three decades earlier. Railroad tracks, long since abandoned, crisscrossed behind its dilapidated, two–story warehouse. A fire had destroyed most of the other buildings, in the sprawling five–acre complex, in the late seventies. Snow, rain, and termites methodically wore away its remnants, leaving behind a crumbling, decaying mess. The warehouse had been a popular hangout for teenagers until Tommy Miller and Johnny Carrington, two Darien High School seniors, lost their lives when a section of the roof fell on top of them during an all night beer blast in the winter of '85.

Four badly weathered walls, precariously held together by a broken–down roof, were all that remained of the Prospect Point Salt Mine and the 500 men that had labored deep within its cavernous belly. The mine sat two miles southeast of the Hinkle farm on top of a hill that gave rise to its name. A single–lane dirt access road wove its way from Route 354 to the front of the warehouse. An old, broken–down, and abandoned delivery truck, its body riddled with bullet holes made by frustrated hunters, lay decaying to the left of the warehouse's huge garage door. Two fresh ruts parted the deep snow that blanketed the access road.

Jimmy eased up on the throttle and pulled the snowmobile alongside a pumping station that was a dozen feet off the road. The warehouse was thirty yards further down the road. The cold drizzle turned into a light snow as the clouds drew thicker. Dozens of blackbirds, huddled on an overhead powerline, cast a foreboding shadow.

"They should be coming along shortly," the Sheriff announced as he dismounted from the snowmobile.

Corey pumped the shotgun and laid the barrel across a cement block that supported two 18–inch steel pipes. "You sure they've got to come this way?"

"Yep, you can't get out of the valley without passing by us. They'll be along." A stiff breeze picked up and swirled across their backs. "The road winds along the mountain and dips into a tunnel for a stretch, before spilling out just east of the Hinkle farm. They can't be but a mile away at best. They should pop into sight any second now."

"What's that building?" Corey asked, pointing to the warehouse. He pulled his collar tight, trying in vain to keep the wet snow off his neck.

"That's Prospect Point Salt Mine's old warehouse…or what's left of it. The mine was Darien's biggest employer for more than fifty years." Jimmy wiped the drizzle from his forehead. "It closed down the summer I left for 'Nam. Three out of four tunnels flooded and the fourth dried–up. They squeezed as much salt out of her as they could before calling it quits. Most town folks had a relative that worked there at one time or another. Some, including my wife's father, were lucky enough to collect a pension. Most had to find jobs elsewhere. Darien never really recovered."

"I've lived in D.C. all my life. Everybody works for the government. You never have to worry about finding a job. It's easy to forget about small town America there. Especially when you're sitting behind a desk, pushing papers for a living."

"Yep, I suppose it is. Lord knows we have our share of problems out here, but you can leave your door open after the sun goes down and still get a good night's sleep. I'll take that over city living every time."

"I can't tell you the last time I left my door open at—"

"We've got company," Jimmy interrupted. He tapped Corey on the shoulder and pointed as the white van bounced into view. "Right on schedule. Do you mind if I borrow that shotgun? Its site can be a little finicky and we may only get one shot at this." Jimmy handed over his Beretta and swung the shotgun across the cement support."

Corey slipped the clip out of the Beretta and examined it before sliding it back into place. "I'm a pistol man myself," he said, trying hard to mask his nervousness.

The van cleared the turn and chugged up the hill towards the pumping station. Jimmy's heart raced. Short puffs of breath escaped into the cold air. His hands tightened on the rifle. He slid the safety off and placed a finger on the trigger. In the brief moment before the van came into range he thought of Ed Ryan and Joe Morgan's lifeless bodies and the pain etched in Nattie's face. He thought of young Mark Coleman sitting in a wheelchair, staring out his bedroom window, watching his friends skateboarding in the street. Finally he thought of his wife, her gentle smile and comforting voice. He thought of the smell of her perfume, touch of her hand, and feel of her lips. A single tear escaped from his eye and rolled down his cheek as he brought the van into his sights.

"This is for you, Anne," he whispered.

CHAPTER 11

Slater leaned back and turned his head toward the back of the van. "You didn't happen to bring along any cold ones, did you, bro?"

"No, but we'll have plenty of time for that after we get out of this friggin' place. We've got to get across the border before it gets too hot around here. They'll seal the borders after they realize what happened," Baker answered. "We need to beat the pricks to the punch."

"Damn, I haven't had a brewski in over a year," Slater replied, licking his lips. "Man, what I wouldn't give for a cold beer and a blowjob. And not necessarily in that order."

Robinson turned and laughed. "I like 'em both at the same time...nothing as sweet as a little head with my beer. Umm...umm...umm! Can't get me enough of that."

"Not to worry, Jack. I'll hook you up with both just as soon as we—"

Jimmy calmly squeezed the trigger and got off a round. It exploded from the barrel in a loud bang that echoed like thunder through the valley. The slug tore into the front tire and sent the van careening out of control, churning up thick waves of blackened slush as it slid across the slippery mountain road. Robinson strangled the steering wheel, struggling to gain control as the van slid sideways towards a drainage ditch. Slush crashed against the windshield, leaving Robinson gasping for even the slightest glimpse of the road.

Jimmy squeezed off another two rounds before Baker and his crew knew what hit them. The second round exploded the passenger side window, launching shards of glass deep into Slater and Robinson's faces, turning them into bloody ribbons of flesh. The third round bore through the van's thin metal door, piercing it like a tin can. The slug ricocheted through Slater's upper torso, slicing his heart and lungs before exiting, in a bloody mass, through his shoulder. His body twisted and heaved. He moaned and slumped forward, hitting his head hard against the dashboard. His eyes rolled back and he lost consciousness. Blood poured from his body, quickly coloring the floorboards with a gooey bloody hue. It streamed from his nose and mouth, choking back his last remaining breaths.

Baker and Peterson's bodies thrashed back and fourth in the belly of the van as it swerved wildly across the road. Baker's head crashed into a metal footlocker, knocking the wire–rimmed sunglasses from his face and tearing a four–inch gash across his forehead. A tire iron slid across the floor, smashing hard into Peterson's foot, shattering three of his toes.

Corey rose to his feet and peppered the vehicle with half of a clip. Bullets flooded the rear of the van, ricocheting in every direction. They whizzed past Baker, just inches from his head. He could feel the breeze left by their wake. Slices of sunlight filtered in through the holes they left in the van's metal shell.

Two bullets found their mark, slicing deep into Peterson's leg. One split his thigh nearly in half, the other passed cleanly through his lower leg, bringing with it most of his calf. Sharp, excruciating pain exploded up his spine. Blood quickly soaked his pants and filled his boot.

"I'M HIT! I'M FUCKING HIT. OH JESUS, IT HURTS!" Peterson screamed.

The wipers cleared the slush from the windshield just in time for Robinson to turn the wheel, keeping it from tumbling into the ditch.

Streams of blood and sweat rained down his forehead and face, spilling into his eyes.

GET TO THE WAREHOUSE!" Baker yelled. "GET TO THE GOD DAMN WAREHOUSE!" He rose to his feet and staggered to the back window amid the chaos, stepping over Peterson's reeling body. He smashed the glass with the butt of his rifle and fired his AK–47 blindly towards the pumping station, buying Robinson precious seconds.

Corey and Taggert ducked behind the safety of the concrete wall and reloaded. The pinging of bullets ricocheting off the steel pipes sounded surreal, like hail on a tin roof. Robinson righted the van and turned down the road leading to the warehouse. Its tires plowed furiously through the wet snow, spitting it out in long plumes, leaving a cloud of white in its wake. It bounced violently, bottoming out as it sped down the rough road. Baker jammed his hand in his coat, fumbling frantically for another clip, tossing the spent one out the window.

Jimmy stood, pumped the shotgun, took aim, and fired. The slug caught Robinson in his upper back, just above the edge of the seat. It tore through his body, ripping his insides before exploding from his chest and lodging deep in the door. Pieces of flesh and bone spattered the windshield, slowly sliding down to the dashboard, leaving a grisly trail. His left arm and leg went numb. Blood–soaked his shirt and jacket. Still, he managed to make it to the warehouse, crashing the bullet–riddled van through its weathered door, before slumping forward and watching helplessly as blood left his body in spurts. Less than two minutes passed before he lost consciousness, less than five before he lost his life.

Baker grabbed Peterson, dragged him from the van, and laid him alongside the warehouse door while holding his AK–47 in one hand and returning fire. Spent shells flew rapidly from his rifle, quickly littering the cedar plank floor. Peterson clutched a pistol in each hand, shooting blindly out the door. Blood continued to ooze from his legs, slowly seeping through the warped floorboards.

Baker took off his belt and wrapped it tightly around Peterson's leg, trying desperately to slow the blood loss. Blood from the gash to his forehead trickled down the side of his face, spilling onto his collar, spattering his coat.

"Danny and Jack?" Peterson asked.

Baker shook his head. "They didn't make it," he said in a quiet, barely audible voice.

Peterson turned away and closed his eyes. "I told you I had a bad feeling about this job. We should have left this shit–hole days ago." He pulled himself up, resting his back against the wall. A cold draft wrapped itself around his neck, sending a shiver down his spine. "It don't look good, huh?" he asked, struggling to catch his breath.

"I've seen worse," Baker replied, forcing a slight smile. "It'll be a while before you dance again." Blood was still surging, unabated, from the leg. Peterson's color worsened and he began to quiver.

"I can't believe it's gonna end here…in this fucking place. Christ, who'd have believed it? We've had half the goddamn FBI looking for us at one time or another and we end up getting ripped by a small town cop," he shook his head and coughed. "It would be funny if I wasn't laying here bleeding to death," he said, feigning a smile. "Taggert's one tough son–of–a–bitch. I'll give the old man that much." He reached up pulled Baker close. "You gotta go, man. You gotta get out of here. The van's toast. You've got no wheels and you sure as hell can't carry me. Go on. Get out of here. Go before it's too late."

"I'm not leaving you. No way. Not a chance."

"Get me a det cord. Run it up to the explosives and leave me to finish this. Leave me to finish Taggert." Peterson wiped the sweat from his brow and swallowed hard. "There's a trap door, that leads to a tunnel, by that old potbelly stove in the corner. The tunnel runs underground for a few hundred yards. There's an airshaft that branches off the main passage after the first hundred yards or so.

You'll know it when you see it. It's a tight fit for the first few yards but it opens up after that. Anyway, it comes out on the other side of the mountain. The evergreen trees are thick there, they'll give you plenty of cover."

"How do you know about the tunnel?" Baker asked.

"I snooped around when you and Danny were out looking for the van."

Baker looked over his shoulder at the area in front of the stove. "I'll take you with me. We'll both go."

"I ain't going nowhere," Peterson snarled. He looked down at his leg and back up again at Baker. "We both know I'm not gonna make it. I've lost too much blood already and I'm sure as hell not gonna die in a tunnel. I'm a soldier. Remember? I'll go down fighting. Do what you gotta do. I'd leave you behind if it was you sitting here bleeding like a stuck pig." He looked him in the eyes. "You know I would."

Baker glanced at the stove again and turned back toward Peterson. "Yeah, I know. But—"

"But nothing," Peterson snapped, grasping the front of Baker's sweater and pulling him close. "Do me a favor. Will you?"

"Sure, anything...anything at all," Baker replied.

"Finish the job we've been planning. Don't quit on me. I don't want to die for nothing. Do it for me, man." Peterson looked him in the eyes and held out his hand.

Baker squeezed it hard. "It'll get done. I promise. It'll get done just like we planned, Kyle. We'll be famous...you and me. You've got my word."

Peterson's condition quickly deteriorated. His ashen face broke out in a cold sweat, and his body shivered. His hands were cold to the touch. "Good deal. Now grab Holloway's body and toss it in the van. Hurry, before I pass out. That'll leave four bodies. They'll think all of us died in the explosion. All you have to do is stay in the tunnel 'til it gets dark and then find a set of wheels. The border will be clear by then. Cops don't search for dead men."

He fed two fresh clips into his pistols and pulled a lighter from his pocket. "Run a det cord for me after you take care of the drunk's body. Make sure it's wired into all of the stuff. I'll give you as much of a lead as I can but you'd better haul–ass down there. Those beams don't look too fucking sturdy and this blast is really gonna shake up the place. It's really gonna rock!" He opened a can of chewing tobacco and stuffed a wad in his cheek. "Guess I don't have to worry about this shit killing me anymore, huh?"

Jimmy pumped his shotgun and turned toward Corey. "You ready to finish this?" He asked with a determined look on his face.

Corey nodded. "Yeah, I doubt they're going to surrender peacefully, huh? What do have in mind?"

"Lay down a line of fire and I'll try to make it to that beat–up delivery truck to the left of the warehouse door. It'll give me some decent cover and a good shooting angle."

Corey poked his head around the corner of the cement wall, glanced at the delivery truck, and raised an eyebrow. "You sure about this? That's a pretty long haul and you'll be in the open for most of the run."

Jimmy turned and smiled. "I'll make it. I was the second fastest kid in high school."

"I hate to burst your bubble, but that was more than thirty years ago. It's *possible* you may have lost a step or two since then."

Jimmy had a nervous grin on his face. "Yeah, but I didn't have anybody shooting at me back then either."

"You got a point there," Corey replied, and smiled.

"Give me plenty of cover and I'll make it."

"Not a problem. I've got two fresh clips. Just say when."

Jimmy pulled his gloves tight and measured the distance to the truck with his eyes one last time before slowly rising to his feet. "On three. Okay?" he said, taking a deep breath.

Corey looked him in the eye and offered a slight nod. He gripped the Beretta tightly, resting his arm on the top of the cement wall. "You got it. Three it is. Keep moving and don't stop to enjoy the scenery. Okay?"

Baker slowly lowered himself down the wood plank ladder, pausing for a moment to look at Peterson one last time before easing the trap door down, leaving his friend behind. Most of the plank rungs of the ladder were broken or missing, making the 20–foot descent slow and disconcerting. He managed to make it to the ground without falling. He pulled the ladder down and left it on the dirt floor. Cobwebs choked the tunnel. His flashlight beam reflected off their silky surface, illuminating a world of total darkness. Once massive support timbers were now hollow and frail, left twisted and sagging from decades of decay. The air was dank and thick with the stench of rotting wood, stagnant water, and rat droppings, making Baker nauseous and sick. Walls were wet to the touch, and pools of water ebbed between the piles of rubble that covered rusted pushcart tracks. Rats scurried from the light; their frightful squealing resonated throughout the eerie tunnel.

Baker lowered his head, covered his nose and mouth with a forearm, and ran as fast as he could. He stumbled and tripped, scraping his shoulders and head against the jagged walls. He could feel breakfast churning in his stomach. Still, he pushed forward, not taking the time to stop. He retched as he ran, vomit oozed from his mouth and nose, dribbling onto his jacket before spilling onto the ground. Rats darted from shadowy crevices, snatching small chunks of puke and scampering back to their nests to savor their tasty find.

The beam from the flashlight bobbed erratically as he frantically scrambled through the tunnel. A bat darted out from behind a rock, startling him. He turned and swung the flashlight wildly, trying to swat it away. As he turned, he stepped on a loose rock, lost his footing, and tumbled hard to the ground, crashing his shoulder and upper back into a support post. The flashlight flew from his hand, hit the ground, and went dead, thrusting the tunnel in pitch–black darkness.

Baker crawled along the ground in a panic, spitting out mouthfuls of cobwebs. Gravel and wood splinters dug into his knees and hands as he frantically swept the floor for the flashlight. A sharp, cutting pain burned deep between his shoulder blades, exacerbated by each breath he drew. His heart thumped wildly, driving blood rapidly through throbbing arteries. His cold sweat dripped on the floor. He could hear the sounds of rats scampering nearby, inching closer, no longer having the light to fear. He pictured the wretched animals in his mind, hunched back on their hind legs, whiskers twitching, nostrils flaring, sniffing the air, exposing their razor sharp teeth before advancing towards him a few inches at a time. He sensed hundreds of beady, cold eyes on him.

Rats don't hunt in packs. Not like dogs, he thought, and prayed.

Their incessant squealing left room for doubt.

He reached and groped in total darkness, banging his outstretched hand against the jagged rocks, tearing and scraping his skin, leaving the inviting scent of fresh blood lingering in the damp air. The walls seemed to be closing in around him and time was quickly running out. Suddenly, without warning, two small teeth tore deep into his calf, ripping away a piece of flesh. He screamed and kicked wildly with his other leg, catching the cat–sized rat in its side and sending it sprawling across the floor, still clutching a piece of his flesh tightly in its clenched jaw. Another rat sprung from a rocky perch, landing squarely on his back. Its pointy claws tore through his sweater, digging into his skin, steadying itself before the attack. Baker screamed and rolled sharply, thrashing his back against the wall, pinning the rat. It let out a piercing shriek before tumbling to the dirt and limping away. Packs of rats moved closer, taking its place, slowly surrounding him. The smell of fresh blood was overwhelming, driving them into a maddening frenzy. He could feel their coarse fur brush up against his body as they scurried past him, positioning themselves for the kill.

Peterson leaned against the wall, holding a det cord firmly in one hand and a lighter in the other. One pistol rested in his lap, the other sat on the floor in a pool of blood. His cheek bulged from a wad of chewing tobacco stuffed up alongside his gum. A steady stream of drool slid down his chin and neck. He hummed a tune from *Bad Company* in his head and desperately struggled to stay awake. "Another minute, that's all I got left, partner. Run...run as fast as you fucking can," he muttered. His breaths were shallow and weak, and he lost all feeling below his waste. He was cold—colder than he ever remembered feeling.

Corey stood and laid down fire as Jimmy sprinted towards the truck. Bullets ripped through the plank siding and ricocheted in the warehouse, pinging off the van and potbelly stove. Splinters of wood flew from the walls.

Peterson turned his head, peering through a narrow crack in the wall, and caught a glimpse of Jimmy streaking up the long, winding road. A smug smile crept up on his face. "That's it, cop...come a little fucking closer," he whispered. "Come on down. It's *show* time!"

Baker's arm brushed up against the flashlight and he quickly closed his hand around it, fumbling for the switch. He frantically flicked it back and forth, holding his breath and praying. Nothing happened. No light—just total darkness. Panic and fear swelled inside, threatening to overwhelm him. "Come on, come on…light you fucking piece of shit," he screamed. A rat ran across his leg, its claws tugged his skin, sending a shiver up his spine. He clutched the flashlight in one hand and smacked it with the other. It produced a spark—a flicker of light—a glimmer of hope. "Goddamn it! Give me a fucking br—" He banged it again and tightened the cap a quarter turn. A beam of light radiated from the flashlight, illuminating the tunnel, casting shadows along its rugged walls. Rats scattered in every direction, slipping into crevices and holes, hiding behind piles of rubble. Their shadows were large on the wall. Baker rose to his feet and fled as fast as his legs would carry him. He was wondering if he was too late. Wondering if the rats were following him. Wondering if he'd die in the tunnel.

Jimmy leapt the last yard and a half to the safety of the truck, bracing his back up against its rusty frame, wondering why no one had shot at him. He flashed a thumb's up sign to his partner while struggling to catch his breath. Puffs of warm air billowed from his lungs, rising high in the air. Corey slid down behind the concrete wall and slipped the last remaining clip into his Beretta.

Peterson spit a brownish string of tobacco drool on the ground, lit the det cord, and turned his head toward the door. "Hey Taggert," he yelled with all the strength he could muster.

"Yeah," Jimmy replied, tightening the grip on his shotgun.

"Can I ask you a question that's been on my mind for a few days?"

"Come out with your hands up and you can ask all the questions you want."

"It's kinda personal, Sheriff." Peterson said coughing and spitting up blood. He watched as the det cord burned slowly across the floorboards, winding its way through the debris that littered the rotting warehouse floor.

"Come out with your hands in the air. I'm not asking again," Jimmy repeated sternly.

The pistol that Peterson held slipped from his feeble grip and fell harmlessly to the floor. He slowly turned his head towards the door. "I was wondering if your wife swallowed or spit it out," he said with a shallow, haunting laugh. "I'm guessing she wasn't the swallowing type. I'm right. Ain't I?"

The det cord reached the van and burned quickly to an olive green backpack tucked under the driver's seat.

Baker wiggled his slender body through the narrow opening. Serrated rocks sliced his skin, leaving him bloody and bruised. The tunnel turned sharply to the left and as he cleared the corner he caught his first glimpse of sunlight. A sense of euphoria and giddiness coursed through his body as he accelerated towards the safety and comfort of the light. Suddenly, he no longer felt the sharp pain with each breath, nor the throbbing headache from the blow to his head, nor the cutting pain of his bloodied calf. The fear that had threatened to consume him dissipated in the briefest of seconds, leaving the rats little more than a distant memory. His lips curled into a broad smile, his white teeth glistened in the dark.

Baker was less than fifty yards from the freedom of the outside world when the explosion thundered through the tunnel. The ground shook violently, knocking him off his feet. Support posts and timbers crumbled, shredding to little more than splinters. The walls buckled and the roof collapsed, starting at one end and cascading to the other. Powerful waves of dust and dirt roared from the warehouse end of the tunnel towards where Baker lay, threatening to bury him alive.

He struggled to his feet and frantically pushed towards the light as the storm cloud rushed to swallow him. The ground rumbled and quaked under his feet, threatening to spill him onto the tunnel's floor once more.

❦ ❦ ❦

The warehouse went up with one large bang. A huge fireball climbed high into the air, raining down sheets of debris, blackening the sky. Corey curled up in the fetal position, tucking his head under his arms. Pieces of the warehouse fell all around him, crashing to the ground.

It took awhile before the dust settled and he was able to emerge from the safety of the concrete wall. A loud ringing in his ears chased his thoughts away. He rose to his feet, slowly surveying the damage. There was nothing left of the warehouse except for a small section of the far corner. Everything else was gone—completely blown away—vaporized in a fraction of a second. His eyes focused on the burnt–out shell of the delivery truck and the pile of rubble that smothered it.

"TAGGERT!" he yelled and ran, pushing quickly through the deep snow.

CHAPTER 12

The airshaft exited on the sunny side of the mountain, surrounded by snow–covered rocks, neatly tucked away in a grove of evergreen trees. Its opening was layered with rubble, choking it off from the outside world. A brilliant falling sun glistened off snow-capped mountains, reflecting in a narrow mountain stream. A red–tailed hawk floated high above, letting the autumn winds carry him across the sun–soaked valley.

Baker lay unconscious, face down in the melting snow, still clutching the flashlight in his hand. The crusty, dried blood on his pant leg left it stiff and hard. A draft of cold air sliced through the valley, swirling along the north ridge before wrapping itself around his bare neck, sending a shiver down his spine. He stirred slowly; his eyes squinted heavily against the setting sun. His memory was little more than a blur.

He gathered himself after a long while and collected his thoughts, slowly remembering the tunnel, the rats, the explosion, and his best friend, Kyle Peterson. He pulled himself up, using a tree to steady wobbly legs. He was tired, hungry, and cold, but waited until nightfall before stepping out of the safety of the trees and heading towards the road. Route 354 curled around an old stone wall before slipping under a railroad bridge a quarter mile down the mountain. A half moon hung low in the sky, just above the tree line. Baker walked along the tracks for several miles before quietly disappearing into the night.

⁂

A day and a half passed before Jimmy regained consciousness. He struggled to open his eyes against the glare of the florescent lights dangling above his bed. A throbbing headache clogged his thoughts and was compounded by the constant ringing in his ears. A dark, fuzzy shadow hovered over him, gradually coming into focus.

"Well, it's about time, Taggert. I was beginning to think you were hibernating for the winter."

Jimmy recognized his voice just as Mitchell Corey's face came into focus. He drew a breath, feeling a deep, cutting pain in his chest. He tried sitting up but couldn't. "Oh man, what the hell happened? My head's pounding. I feel as though I was run over by a truck," he said, grimacing. "Last thing I remember is resting against the delivery truck in front of the warehouse. Waiting to go in."

Corey pulled up a chair and sat down, handing Jimmy a cup of cold water. "Actually, you did get run over by a truck…sort of anyway." He leaned forward, resting his elbows on his knees. "The warehouse went up in flames. They detonated a couple pounds of explosives, enough to level the place. The only reason you're alive is because you were lucky enough to fall into a drainage ditch. The delivery truck rolled on top of you, shielding you from the force of the blast. It took us the better part of four hours to dig you out. I didn't think you'd make it—not looking the way you did when we pulled you out of the rubble. I swear, you must have a horseshoe stuck up your ass, surviving two blasts in one day. Geez!"

"Baker?" Jimmy asked coughing. He gulped down the cup of water and motioned for more. It felt soothing against his parched throat.

"Toast. All of 'em are dead…Robinson, Slater, Peterson and pretty boy—Baker. We found pieces of four bodies in the warehouse. End of the line. Case closed. The bad guys lose…just like in the movies."

Jimmy closed his eyes and sighed, feeling like a ton of weight had been lifted from his shoulders. "I wish it were a movie. Wish none of it ever happened. I keep hoping it's been nothing more than a dream, and that I'll wake up next to my wife in the morning." He turned and looked out the window, staring at a couple walking hand in hand along the river. Reddish–orange leaves cascaded down from maple trees that lined the walkway. A light breeze scattered them across the park. Most ended up piled against a stone wall on the river's edge. "So what are you still hanging around Darien for? Got nothing better to do?" he asked, slowly turning away from the window. His lips curled into a crooked, forced smile.

Corey shook his head and laughed. "I was thinking about settling around here and opening up a coffee shop with Max."

"Christ, don't make me laugh. It hurts too damn much!" Jimmy chuckled. "Max's coffee…I sure as hell don't miss that crap."

"I'll say one thing about it, though. It sure wakes you up in the morning!" Corey smiled and glanced at his watch. "I'm just tying up some loose ends. Still haven't found the rest of the cache of *Generation X*. And now that public enemy number one is dead, we probably never will. I don't like the thought of a few hundred pounds of the stuff lying around somewhere. It scares the hell out of me."

"It'll eventually turn up. Stuff like that usually does. It might be ten years from now, but it'll turn up. Some kids will probably stumble on it. I just hope they don't end up blowing themselves up. How long does it take to degrade?"

"That's the beauty of the stuff. It doesn't degrade at all. It remains incredibly stable. You could bury it for a thousand years. Dig it up. Set a det cord to it and it'll go up with just as much punch as if it were brand spanking new!"

Jimmy swallowed another mouthful of water. The coldness chilled his teeth, making his headache worse. "Wonderful. Who the hell invented the stuff? And more importantly, why?"

Corey shrugged his shoulders. "Probably a lab rat, on a slow Friday afternoon. Had nothing better to do so he passed on the perfect mousetrap and opted for a batch of designer explosives. Probably figured the royalties would be a tad higher."

"So when are you heading back to Washington?" Jimmy asked.

"I'm catching the redeye out of here tonight. I've got to be at the White House for a 6:00 A.M. briefing. Seems we've had a few bomb threats at the Israeli Embassy in the past month and their ambassador is flipping out. He hasn't left the compound for the better part of two weeks, and is getting a tad bit squirrelly, to say the least. So what are you going to do after they let you out of here? Still gonna retire? Take the big easy?"

Jimmy glanced out the window again. "Don't see the point in retiring now…not without Anne. I'd go crazy sitting in my house all day. Too much time to do too much thinking. It'd tear me up inside. No, I suppose I'll be sheriffing for a while longer. At least 'til I find something that will keep me busy."

Corey stood up, buttoned his suit, and straightened his tie. "Well I better be going. I still have a report to write. Have to fax it to the office by five…you know the drill. Take care of yourself and look me up if you ever get to the Capital. I'll show you around town. Might even buy you a beer or two."

"I'll do that. Maybe stop by *The Wall* when I'm down there. Pay my respects to Bobby."

"You're welcome anytime." He shook Jimmy's hand. "It's been a pleasure working with you. Get better soon," he said, and walked out the door.

* * *

Jimmy stepped out of his truck and walked slowly past the neatly trimmed rows of gravestones, clutching a bouquet of wildflowers firmly in his hand. A welcoming sun, surrounded by a sapphire sky, radiated brightly on the cloudless day. It warmed the valley, freeing Darien from an early winter's grip. The warmth of the sun on his face felt soothing, almost therapeutic. He walked to a solitary plot atop a hill, shaded by a towering oak, and knelt down on the broken earth. Spring would be six weeks old before the first blades of grass pushed through the naked soil. Two large urns, filled with red geraniums, flanked his wife's granite headstone. He laid the flowers at the foot of her headstone, took his hat off, and said a silent prayer. His eyes welled and quickly teared. He wiped the wetness away with his sleeve. After a long silent moment he began to speak in a voice that was little more than a whisper.

"I brought your favorite flowers. Stopped by the florist's on the way over here. Old Red wouldn't take a penny for 'em. Said they were scraps…but they weren't. Red never could lie worth a lick. He knew I was bringing 'em out to you."

Jimmy's throat tightened and his voice cracked. "The sun finally broke through. Melted the snow…all of it. Put winter on hold for a while, I suppose. Although you never can tell, huh?" A warm breeze pushed through the cemetery, gently rustling the leaves. A crow swooped down from the top of the tree, roosting on a chapel cross. "I talked with the kids today. Seems little Jimmy's got a case of chicken pox. Debbie said he's scratching like a barn dog in the middle of July. Everyone else is okay. Fit as a fiddle as you used to say. They're getting ready for Thanksgiving. Invited me down. But I can't go," he said shaking his head. "Not this year. Not this soon. I haven't spent a Thanksgiving away from you in thirty years. Not since 'Nam. And I'm not ready to…not this year." He put his head in his hands and sobbed. "I'm sorry. I'm so damn sorry, Anne. If only I'd done something differently. I should have protected you. It should have been me, not you. Please forgive me. Can you ever forgive me? God, I miss you. Think about you all the time…every minute of every day. It hurts. It hurts so damn much."

Jimmy knelt at his wife's grave for a while longer without saying another word. As he rose to his feet he caught a glimpse of someone watching him from the safety of a distant tree, his face hidden by its enormous shadow. An uneasy feeling rose from the pit of the sheriff's stomach, the hairs on the back of his neck stood on end. Just then, the police radio in his truck barked and he turned away. By the time he looked back again, the figure was gone. He walked to the truck and picked up the microphone.

"Taggert," he answered, glancing again at the spot where the figure had stood a moment earlier.

"Sheriff, I'm sorry to bother you on your lunch."

"It's okay, Max. I'm just finishing up. What ya got?"

"We got a call of some trouble over at the McCoy's. Seems the Hatfield twins pissed old Johnny off again and he's looking to pepper their behinds with a load of buckshot. He's got 'em cornered in his barn. The report says they're holding a knife to his prize cow's throat, threatening to make dinner out of the poor thing unless he drops the shotgun. I'd send Richie out on the call but he's tied up on a fender–bender halfway across the county."

"I'm on my way. I'm only a few miles from there. Get a hold of Hank Hatfield and have him meet me at the farm. Give me a couple minutes head start. I don't want him beating me out there. I've got enough to deal with without worrying about old Hank going off, too. You copy, Maximus?"

"I'm on it like white on rice, Sheriff."

"Good. I'll radio in just as soon as I get things settled."

"Sheriff?"

"Yeah, Max. What is it?"

"It's good having you back."

Jimmy smiled. "It's good to be back, Max. It's good to be back."

CHAPTER 13

A brilliant sunset gave way to a moonless night, thick with storm clouds. Wind chimes clanged loudly against howling gusts. Cold, driving rain fell angry on the roof, spilling across the living room's skylight in torrents, as lightning stabbed the sky and thunder rumbled across the valley. Jimmy was sound asleep on the sofa—his bed ever since his wife's death. His legs looked gangly and awkward, crumpled against the worn armrest. A mystery novel lay across his chest, wire–rimmed reading glasses were pushed up on his forehead. He never heard the soft footsteps on his back porch, nor the pocket-knife being wedged between the lockset and doorjamb.

Michael Baker, dressed in black, stepped silently inside Jimmy's house, bringing the wind and rain with him. He gently planted each foot on the tile floor, heel–to–toe. His wet footprints tracked across the breezeway, reflecting in the soft glow of a nightlight, marching towards the kitchen. His heart raced and breath quickened. Hatred coursed through ice–cold veins. Dark, penetrating eyes darted everywhere. He wrapped his fingers tightly around a ten–inch hunting knife. Its razor–sharp blade glistened, slicing through the darkness with each flash of lightning. He choked on anticipation, having rehearsed every step over and over again in his head until they resonated clearly from every corner of his mind. He had waited patiently for the perfect night, hiding in the small thicket of woods just south of the house. Waiting for the wind and rain—waiting for the perfect cover—waiting for his revenge.

After a few minutes, Baker shed his windbreaker, letting it fall silently to the floor, and stepped out from behind the door, slowly entering the living room. His camouflaged hunting boots, still wet with rain, left faint imprints on the polished hardwood floor. He placed each foot down gingerly, letting the soft rubber soles absorb the noise, and crept silently by the fireplace. Its gentle glow cast an eerie shadow against the wall. The floorboards gently moaned under his weight as he slithered, undetected, across the length of the room.

He approached the sofa from behind, holding the knife out in front of him. Black leather gloves were pulled tight to his skin. Short shoots of blonde hair slipped out from underneath the baseball cap he wore backwards on his head. He took a deep breath and cleared the last several feet in one fluid motion. His hand clamped down hard on the Sheriff's mouth. He thrust the edge of the knife against his throat. Its point tugged forcefully at his skin. Jimmy's eyes shot open wide and his body shuddered. Lightening flashed, illuminating Baker's chilling smile.

"You look like you've just seen a ghost, Sheriff," Baker grinned.

The taste of wet leather made Jimmy gag. His heart raced and muscles tensed. A shiver ran down his spine.

Baker pushed harder against the knife. Blood began to trickle along its edge, slowly sliding down Taggert's neck and dripping onto the sofa. Jimmy felt the cold steel against his clammy skin. Its serrated edge threatened to cut through the thin layer of cartilage lining his throat. "Nothing quite like the fear that a knife conveys," he said in a raspy whisper. "Don't you think? Guns are too impersonal…too sterile for my taste. Call me old–fashioned, but I prefer it up close and personal. Like to get my hands *dirty*, so to speak." Baker leaned forward until he was inches from Jimmy's face. His breath reeked of whiskey and cigarettes. Sweat ran off his nose, dripping onto the sheriff's forehead. "I like to hear the last gasp of air rushing from someone's throat after I slit it. It makes such a fascinating gurgling sound. You know what I mean…don't you? Blood rushing in as air's rushing out. It gets me high. Gets the juices flowing. There's nothing like it," he said, wetting his lips with his tongue and smiling. "Absolutely *nothing* like it."

"I love to see people panic. See the fear in their eyes. You know the kind of fear I'm talking about. They know they're going to die and they can't do a thing about it. The same fear I'm seeing in your eyes right now. He pushed the knife deeper as he leaned closer. "You shouldn't have tried to be a hero. This isn't like the movies where the good guys always win. You should have let us leave your back–ass town. No one would have gotten hurt. Baker's grin turned to a scowl and his eyes narrowed. "You shouldn't have killed Kyle."

He lifted the knife high above his head and plunged it deep into Jimmy's chest.

CHAPTER 14

Max Wakefield burst into the Sheriff's office, sending the door crashing into the plaster wall as Jimmy's second scream echoed through the room.

Jimmy was sitting upright in his chair, eyes shut tight. His face was flushed and covered with a blanket of sweat. His chest heaved with rapid breaths and his body shuddered.

"SHERIFF!" Max yelled.

There was no response.

Max clutched the Sheriff's shoulders. "JIMMY…JIMMY!" he yelled, shaking him hard.

Jimmy sprung from his chair, grabbed Max, and threw him against the wall. Instinctively, he drew back his arm and clenched his hand into a tight fist.

Max covered his face, bracing himself for the blow. His glasses sat cockeyed on his nose and his hat lay crumpled on the floor. "Jimmy! Jimmy! You're dreaming again. Wake up. It's me…Max. Wake–up!"

Jimmy's eyes shot open wide and he stepped back on wobbly legs, not quite sure of where he was.

Max cautiously lowered his guard and rose to his feet as the Sheriff collected himself.

Jimmy slumped into his chair, burying his face deep into his hands. "I'm sorry, Max. I'm so sorry. I didn't—"

Max straightened his glasses, brushed off his pants, and slid his hat back on his head. He fixed its crease by running his pudgy index finger along its ridge. “Don’t worry about it, Sheriff. I’m no worse for the wear. I’ve got plenty of padding,” he joked. An uneasy smile crossed his face.

“Son–of–a–bitch,” Jimmy moaned. His voice was weak and quivering. “Christ. I was dreaming that Baker was in my house. He came up from behind me while I was sleeping on the couch. Took a knife and drove it into my chest. Jesus! It was so real. It was so damn real.”

Max looked over his shoulder and closed the door behind him. Atwater and Thompson stood by the water cooler, trying hard not to stare.

“Baker’s dead, Chief. He died in the explosion at the mine. I don’t know why you’re having these dreams, but this is the third one in less than a month. You can’t let go of him, for some reason or another.”

Max looked away while nervously tugging on an ear. “We’ve been friends a long time, Jimmy. I know I’m not what most would consider *deputy sheriff material.* I may be book smart but I’m no ball of fire in the field. I hear the talk around town. Still, you always treated me fair. Treated me like one of the guys. Made me feel like I fit in. You’ve always looked out for me and I appreciate that. In all these years I never had a bit of advice for you ‘cause I never saw a time when you might have needed some.” Max paused for a moment, measuring Jimmy’s receptiveness.

“But I do now. I’m not what you’d call a real big believer in shrinks but I think you might want to consider spending some time on a couch. My wife’s cousin swears by ‘em. She’s been going for as long as I can remember. Says it helps to talk about stuff every once in a while.” Max glanced up, tucked his hands deep into his pockets, and shrugged his shoulders. “I don’t know. Maybe it would help for you to talk with someone. Get whatever’s bothering you out of your head. Sometimes things get to rattling around in a man’s head. It can drive you to drink or worse.”

Jimmy looked up and ran his fingers slowly through his hair. "I never felt the need to talk to anyone 'bout my problems, Max. Kept 'em to myself mostly. And when I needed to do some talking I always had Anne. Now she's gone and it's just me and the four walls. It's the quiet that gets to me most. Anne could yak with the best of 'em. She'd drive me crazy half the time. Always wanting to talk to me. Sometimes 'bout nothing at all. Christ! I bet I never got through half of a football game without her wanting to jabber 'bout something or someone." The faint smile that rose on Jimmy's face disappeared as quickly as it came. "Believe it or not, I miss her chatter the most. Miss poking fun of her." His upper lip quivered and eyes welled. He drew a deep breath, exhaling slowly. "Maybe you're right, Max. Maybe I need a bit of help." He feigned a smile and rose to his feet. "I suppose it's time to get to work, huh?"

Max smiled back. "I suppose so," he agreed, turning toward the door.

Jimmy caught him before he had a chance to turn the knob. "Max?" he said.

"Yeah."

"Don't go believing everything you hear on the streets. You're as fine a lawman as there is. We come in all shapes and sizes. Each brings something different to the table. I wouldn't trade you for a litter of the State's finest. We couldn't get by without you."

Max's grin stretched across his round face. "Thanks for saying so, Sheriff. It means a lot coming from you."

"I'm the one that needs to be thanking you."

Max offered a slight nod. "You want the door closed?"

"Nope. Leave it open. I've got a job to do."

CHAPTER 15

Summer, 1999

Jimmy swung his truck sharply into the Ryans' gravel driveway, pushing a cloud of dirt high into the humid summer air. A 24–foot U–Haul truck was backed up to Nattie's front door. A half dozen men loaded a lifetime of living into its cavernous belly. Jimmy jumped from the cab and rushed to the porch. He cradled a box of doughnuts underneath an arm while precariously juggling a piping hot cup of coffee with the other. He grimaced as it spilled out the hole in the lid, singeing his skin. His gray hair was stuffed up under a red baseball cap. A plain white t–shirt was tucked into a beltless pair of blue jeans. The Ryans' yellow Labrador Retriever came bounding around the corner, pushing the side yard's gate open with its wet nose. Its tail wagged a mile a minute and its tongue hung over his yellow teeth. It raced to Jimmy, almost knocking him off his feet.

"Whoa! Take it easy, Cooper…take *it* easy! You're looking as good as new, boy. Aren't ya? Yeah. As good as new."

Nattie stood on the porch, arms folded across her chest. Unforgiving eyes greeted him with an icy stare. She waited for him to hit the first of six painted wood steps before slowly lifting an arm and looking at her watch. "You told me you'd be here a hour and a half ago. All the others got here on time. They had quite a breakfast spread waiting for ‘em. Scrambled eggs, bacon, cinnamon raison bread, and a stack of pancakes half a foot tall. Course they were here on time. I didn't have to keep their plates warm like I did yours. Even Sam Barton got here before you. Last time that happened, Jesus was in diapers."

Jimmy shook his head and laughed out loud. "Top of the morning to you, too," he joked. "It's been one hell of a morning. Let me tell ya, Mrs. R. One hell of a morning, all right."

"Well don't waste time jabbering about it out there. Come in the kitchen and I'll fix you up something. A man can't work on an empty stomach. Least that's what I've been told. Besides, I've seen you in the kitchen and you have trouble making toast. Only the good Lord knows what you're eating now that you're fixin' your own food." Nattie turned and walked in the house, still talking to herself as she entered the kitchen.

"Morning, boys!" Jimmy said, stepping onto the porch. The floorboards moaned under his weight.

"It's about time," Atwater complained, wiping the sweat off his forehead. "We could use an extra pair of hands. It's hotter than hell this morning. My shirt's soaking wet," he added, lifting it in Jimmy's direction. "I've never seen so many boxes before. The house is jammed packed with ‘em. I bet the old lady never threw out a thing her whole life."

"You live in the same house most of your life and you see how much clutter you have after sixty years." Jimmy remarked.

Atwater picked up another box off the porch and stuffed it into the truck. "I ain't gonna have this much shit," he grumbled. "No friggin' way! You've got my permission to shoot me if I ever do. Shoot me right between the eyes and put me out of my misery."

"What happened this morning, Sheriff?" Steve Thompson asked. "Anything going on?"

"Max got hold of me just I was pulling out of my driveway heading this way. Seems there was a break–in at a construction site on

Route 24, across from the textile mill. A case and a half of dynamite is missing. I had to call in the ATF. They're handling the case now. The investigator thinks it was a bunch of kids with too much time on their hands. ATF figures there'll be more than a few stumps blown up the next few weeks." Jimmy paused, taking time to sip his coffee. "I think the ATF is barking up the wrong tree."

"Why's that?" Thompson asked. Two boxes were stuffed up under his muscular arms.

"Who ever it was took the blasting caps too. They ransacked the place looking for 'em. They weren't easy to find. Ed Haley had 'em hid real good. Stashed 'em behind a file cabinet drawer. How many teenagers you suppose know anything about blasting caps? And how many are gonna stick around long enough to find 'em?" Jimmy lifted the hat off his head and ran his fingers through his hair. "No sir. Who ever broke in knew what they were doing...and just what they were lookin' for. They weren't kids. That's for sure. Oh well," he said shrugging his shoulders. "It's not my case—not anymore. Still, something's fishy. I can feel it in my bones." He opened the screen door and was about to step inside when Sam Barton spoke up.

"Hey, Sheriff. Hold on a cotton–pickin' minute."

"Yeah. What is it?"

"Don't be going in the house toting that box of doughnuts you got stuffed up under your arm. I can smell them from here. Bet you got a couple of peanut sticks in there...maybe more."

Jimmy handed the box to Sam and laughed. "You've got a hell of nose for a barber. There *were* two peanut sticks in there...'til I ate one of 'em. Here you go. Knock yourself out," he said. "I'll be out in a few minutes. Why don't you fellas take ten? You're looking kinda ragged."

Atwater rested his lanky body against the truck's bumper, reached into a blue cooler, and pulled out a cold beer. "That's awful nice of you, Sheriff. I can't say I recall who put you in charge, though," he teased.

"I guess you didn't get the memo, huh?" Jimmy shot back before turning and walking into the house. Cooper was a step behind with his nose to the floor. "Hey Nattie. You're working these guys like dogs. Their tongues are dragging. You'd better lighten up a bit, otherwise you're likely to have a strike on your hands."

Nattie scooped a steaming spoonful of scrambled eggs onto a blue plate already crowded with bacon and sausages. "There, that should hold you over 'til lunch," she said, placing the plate on the table.

"That should hold me over 'til lunchtime tomorrow! So much for my low cholesterol diet. You got enough fat in here to choke a pig."

"I bet you'll eat every spoonful though," Nattie said, and smiled.

"I bet you're right. On a good day my breakfast consists of a bowl of cereal and cup of coffee. The closest I come to eggs is an Egg McMuffin at McDonalds' drive–thru."

Jimmy looked around the kitchen. Everything was off the walls, and boxes lined the counter. The cupboards were nearly bare. Newspaper covered the windows. Her hutch and dining room table were loaded on the truck. "I can't imagine anyone else living here. Not after all these years."

Nattie looked at him and then turned away, working on the pile of dishes stacked neatly in the sink as she talked. "I always thought one of the kids would take the house someday. Figured a Ryan would always live here. Selling it to strangers never crossed my mind." She looked out the window above the sink, stealing a peek through the sections of newspaper taped to the glass. Bright sunlight sliced through the gap, cascading across the room. "We had a lot of good memories here. A lifetime's worth. They come with me. I'll always have them to hold onto, no matter where I am," she sighed. "But the house is too big for me. It's too much work for one person. It was getting too much for Ed, even though he'd never admit it. It's not the same without him." She squirted some detergent in the sink and ran the faucet before turning around and sitting at the table. "If I tell you something will you promise not to think I'm a crazy old hag? And that you won't tell anyone else…especially not Sam Barton. That man's mouth is always moving. When he ain't chewing…he's talking. When he ain't talking…he's chewing."

Jimmy smiled slightly and looked up. "I'd never think of you as being crazy, Nattie. I can't say that for most around here but I can for you. You're as solid as a rock. I won't tell a soul. You have my word on it. Now what's on your mind?"

Nattie offered a faint smile and nodded. She lowered her head, keeping her eyes glued to the table. An unfamiliar uneasiness settled in around her. She began to speak in a voice that was little more than a whisper. The words came slowly. "The other day, I dozed off on the couch. It wasn't for too long…a half–hour…maybe forty–five minutes. Couldn't have been much more than that cause I woke up before the evening news. Anyhow, just as I was coming to, I swear I heard Bobby and Ed's voices coming from the back room. I was awake…no doubt about it. Sure as I'm sitting here with you," she hesitated for a moment, looking deep into Jimmy's eyes. "I couldn't quite make out what they were saying but it sounded like they were talking to one another. Carrying on a conversation about something or other. It's strange how you remember a voice for so long. I haven't heard Bobby's in more than thirty years and I can still remember it like it was yesterday. The voices didn't spook me none. To tell you the truth, they were comforting. I wanted them to last longer, but they faded to a whisper and were gone as quickly as they came. I tried closing my eyes and falling back asleep. Figured that might help. But it didn't. That happened a week ago Tuesday. Haven't heard anything since."

Nattie's frail eyes welled and her voice cracked. "There was a time when I was afraid of dying. Not anymore," she said shaking her head. "Don't get me wrong. I'm not looking to go right yet, and don't worry, I'm not planning on doing something stupid. But I don't worry about not waking up in the morning. I skip over that prayer when I hit my knees at night. Figure my time will come soon enough. The good Lord will call me when he sees fit. I'm glad Bobby's not alone. Glad to know he's got someone to talk to."

Jimmy stood and walked over to Nattie. He knelt down alongside of her and held her tight in his arms. "Next time you hear from Bobby you make sure you tell him I said hello. Ask him if he'll look after Anne 'til I get there."

Nattie smiled. Her cheeks were wet with tears. "Look at me, will you? I'm crying like a baby." She leaned forward and kissed Jimmy's cheek. "I guess we still have some work to do, huh?"

"Yes, ma'am. There's a ton of boxes left to load. I suppose the crew's had long enough of a break. Don't you?"

"I suppose so. I better get the dishes washed or we won't have anything to eat lunch on."

"Well, I better get out there and lend a hand. Thanks for the breakfast, Mrs. R. It was delicious as usual. Good thing I didn't wear a belt this morning."

"Jimmy? There's something I've been meaning to mention to you."

"What is it?"

"I was packing up things in Bobby's room the other day and noticed that some of his personal papers were missing."

"What exactly was missing?" Jimmy asked.

"His birth certificate and social security card."

"Anything else?"

"Not so far as I could tell."

Jimmy thought for moment. "Do you know if they were missing before Baker was in the house?"

"I don't know. I never checked. Why? What could he have wanted them for?"

CHAPTER 16

Spring, 2000

The Niagara River curled around Prospect Point, a stone's throw from the small roadside motel that butted up tight against a weathered breakwall. Ashen gray clouds hugged the frigid water, pushing a light morning fog over the river's steep banks. Strong currents carried an ice field down river towards Niagara Falls. Large chunks of ice, some the size of cars, bobbed between tall whitecaps. A flock of seagulls dotted the gloomy sky.

Michael Baker leaned forward in his chair. His elbows rested on the knees, steadying the binoculars he held firmly in his hands. A pencil was sandwiched between his teeth, and a can of soda stood just within reach on the painted windowsill. A pad of paper, cluttered with notes and sketches, lay on a nearby table. The unmade bed was strewn with photographs and reference books, some opened, others with bookmarks wedged tightly between the pages. He studied the ice flow, watching as it crashed into massive concrete piers that supported the Peace Bridge. He studied the bridge's complex structure, its miles of interwoven I–beams, girders, trusses, and steel decking. A construction crew worked tirelessly on its underbelly, huddling on scaffolding hung over its side. Frigid gusts pushed the workers tight to the bridge, pinning them against the cold steel.

Baker rose to his feet, tucked the pencil behind an ear, and unraveled a faded blueprint; handwritten notes were scribbled in its margins. He studied the blueprints carefully, looking up occasionally at the bridge, stopping to check a measurement. He noted it on paper filled with rows of calculations.

"YOU DAMN WELL BETTER HAVE THAT STEEL HERE BY THE MORNING," Sean Mahoney yelled, slamming the phone down while blurting out a string of obscenities. He stood up abruptly, pacing the length of the small construction trailer in just ten short steps. A thick, layered beard covered much of his ruddy face. His balding red hair, brush–cut short, was covered by a yellow hardhat. *MAHONEY* was scrawled, unevenly, in thick black letters across its front. *THE BOSS*, just below it and, "If you can read this you're kissing too much ass" was written in fine print on the back. He was a mountain of a man, six–five and two hundred seventy–five pounds. His red flannel shirtsleeves were rolled up to his elbows, exposing a white thermal undershirt. A black leather belt strangled his potbelly. He took the hat off, throwing it hard into the wall, leaving a deep crack in a wall full of deep cracks.

Michael Baker knocked on the trailer door and stepped inside before being invited.

"What do you want?" Mahoney asked gruffly. His face was still red with anger.

Baker stepped forward, extending his hand. "I'm looking for work. I hear you're *the man*."

"I don't know who you've been speaking to, but I've got a full crew. We're on schedule. I'm not looking to pick up anyone else. Looks like you wasted a trip out here," Mahoney said, bending over and picking his hardhat off the floor. "Now if you don't mind I've got a ton of work to get to this morning."

Baker walked past Mahoney to the window and looked up at the Peace Bridge. "She sure is beautiful. Isn't she? All 3,580 feet of her. Did you know it was the longest non–suspension bridge built at the time? Most thought it couldn't be constructed because of Niagara's currents. The currents are stronger at that stretch of the river than anywhere else."

"My grandfather helped build that bridge seventy–five years ago. Built it with blood and sweat. He was only 16 when he came over from Ireland. He and his brother stowed away on a freighter to New York. They worked their way west on the Erie Canal and eventually settled in Buffalo. They were happier than pigs–in–shit when they landed work on the bridge. Three–fifty an hour…thought they had died and gone to heaven. No one made that kind of money in '25. 'Course they never knew how dangerous the work was and no one bothered to tell 'em. They were just two immigrants looking to get a leg up. Looking for a break. Granddad lost his brother less than a month into the job. Seems the scaffolding he was working on gave way. They found his body down river…a mile past the Falls. Maid–of–the–Mist fetched it out of the water the next day."

Baker paused, still staring at the bridge. "Granddad worked like a dog to get the bridge done on time. Figured he owed it to his brother. Sort of a tribute…or monument, I suppose. He passed on a little more than a month ago. I saw on the news that the bridge was getting a facelift for her anniversary and wanted to lend a hand. Touch the same steel my grandfather did. Sort of a tribute to him you could say." He turned toward Mahoney. A tear slid down his cheek "It'd sure mean a lot to me. I've worked with iron and steel for 15 years. You could say it's in my blood. It don't matter what I do. So long as it has something to do with her," he said pointing to the bridge.

Mahoney ran his fingers across his short hair and scratched his beard. "Tell you what I can do," he said after a moment. "I've got a list of ten men who walked in here ahead of you. All looking for work. I'll put your name first and give you a call if we're behind schedule, or if one of the crew quits on me. I'm not promising anything. The work's hard but, the pay's good. Leave me your name and number and I'll call if anything turns up. That's about the best I can do for you."

Baker smiled and stepped forward. "The name's Ryan...Bobby Ryan. I'm staying at the flea–bag motel on the point just around the bend."

"The place with the burned out sign?"

"That'd be it. It's so bad that even the cockroaches left."

Mahoney laughed loudly. "I've stayed in a few motels like that in my day. You sleep with one eye open, I'll bet."

"If you sleep at all!"

"Ryan, huh? Funny, you don't look too Irish to me."

"Yeah, that's what everyone tells me. My granddad married an English girl and my Mom's German. But I bleed green and I drink like an Irishman," Baker smiled, and winked.

Mahoney laughed again. "That's all that matters."

"Ain't that the truth."

"I'll give you a holler if anything turns up. You got my word on it, Ryan."

"Fair enough. I can't ask for more than that. Thanks for your time."

Baker walked out the door and down the driveway. "What a friggin' sucker," he said shaking his head. "That pig bought the story, hook, line and sinker. And they say Pollacks are stupid! I'll be doing the world a favor when I kill him. It'll improve the gene pool. I hope the fat bastard hasn't reproduced yet. Oh man, is this gonna be easy! Like taking candy from a baby."

CHAPTER 17

Michael Baker sat at the far corner of the bar with a tumbler full of *Jack Daniels* cradled in his hand. He rolled the glass back and forth between his forefinger and thumb, watching the whiskey curl along its beveled edge. Overhead, a wobbly fan pushed stale smoke along the water–stained ceiling. Danny's Corner Bar and Grill was little more than a hole in the wall, but folks came from miles for a taste of Danny's beef on weck. His imported Irish stout and collection of scantily dressed cocktail waitresses didn't hurt business either. Cigarette butts filled the glass ashtray Baker shared with the bartender, a Gulf War veteran named Johnny Rogers.

It was just past six on a Friday evening—payday for Mahoney's bridge crew. Baker watched as they filed in and filled the bar. He sat silently with his back against the wall, nursing his whiskey. Cold penetrating eyes studied the blue–collar men. Some played pool, some sat at the bar. Others groped the hard–bodied waitresses. Each would drink more than a day's pay before the ringing of the last call bell.

"Fill 'er up again?" Johnny asked, leaning over the bar with a bottle of whiskey in his grubby hand. A spent cigar was wedged tightly in the corner of his mouth, jutting from his thick scraggly beard. A solid blue bandanna covered most of his balding forehead, long brown hair was tied back in a ponytail. Powerful forearms were colored red and blue with tattoos. His dark brown eyes rested on padded bags of flesh.

"Yeah, catch me again, Johnny. Give me a double. Will ya?" Baker replied.

Johnny grinned and smiled, exposing a mouthful of missing teeth. The few that remained were little more than cracked yellow–brown pegs. "Here you go. Just what the doctor ordered."

Baker opened his mouth wide and downed the drink with one long gulp. The whiskey burned and made his eyes water. "Hit me again," he said, pushing the empty glass towards the bartender. "And pour yourself one, while you're at it. I don't like drinking alone. Don't be shy. Fill it to the top." He struck a blue tip against the bar and lit a cigarette while Johnny poured another round. "Looks like you've got a bar full of construction workers. What's the deal? Where they from?"

"They're working on the Peace Bridge. Have been for close to a year. They're getting it ready for the big celebration this summer," Johnny answered.

"What celebration would that be?"

"She turns seventy–five this July. There's a big party being planned. Even the fucking President's suppose to come. I don't see what the big deal is. The bridge looks pretty friggin' ugly to me. But I ain't complaining. The crew's been coming in here every Friday night for a year. Those stupid bastards get all liquored up and spend a shit–load of money on booze and broads. I do *real* good in tips. I bet I made close to two hundred bucks last Friday. It used to take me a month of Fridays to pull in that kinda scratch. Shit! I never take a Friday off anymore. And I don't plan to either. Not as long as they're driving steel out there on the Niagara."

Larry Mehan stumbled out of the bar ten minutes after last call, the last member of Mahoney's crew to hit the street. His drunken gait was uneven and exaggerated, exacerbated by the parking lot's loose gravel. His dark blue Impala sat at the far edge of the lot, underneath a freshly broken light. He muttered incoherently as he rolled his fat body into the front seat, stuffing his hands deep into his pockets, probing for his keys. A steady stream of drool ran from the corner of his mouth. The engine sputtered, threatening to quit before turning over in a loud roar. He thrust the car into drive and sped away, clouds of gravel and dirt rose in his wake. Black smoke billowed from the tailpipe and his headlights quickly disappeared in the murky fog.

Mehan lived alone in a one–bedroom trailer less than two miles from the bar. His only responsibility in life was a Shepard–Retriever mix. He steered the Impala along the winding road, drifting between the centerline and side of the road.

He felt cold steel press against his neck as he turned into his dirt driveway

"Turn your lights off," Baker said from the back seat.

A hand grabbed hold of Mehan's hair and pulled sharply back, snapping his neck against the headrest.

Mehan's dog was on its hind legs with its nose pressed tight to the window, barking at the top of his lungs.

"Wh…wh…what d…do you want?" Mehan asked in a trembling voice. He pulled a wad of money from his pocket and held it up above his head. "Take it. It's all I got. There ain't no need to hurt me. I ain't gonna mess with ya. I won't go to the police. You got my word. Take the money and leave."

"Relax. I don't want your money, pal." Baker looked over his shoulder. The road was dark in either direction. He glanced at the trailer. "What's your dog's name?"

Mehan swallowed hard, trying to draw spit into a dry mouth. "Lucky," he murmured. "His name's Lucky."

Baker laughed out loud. "Lucky, huh? Too bad I can't say the same for you."

CHAPTER 18

Mitchell Corey stepped out of the Leer jet, shading his eyes from the morning's bright sun as he headed quickly into the terminal. "Go ahead and get a rental. I've got to make a call. I'll catch up to you in a few minutes," he said, stepping inside the gate.

Rookie FBI agent John Mackey waved and kept walking at a brisk clip.

"Don't get another compact either. You do and I'm sticking *your* ass in the backseat. See how you like having your knees crammed into your chest. Nothing smaller than a Taurus," Corey yelled, snapping open his cellphone and sitting down in a row of seats across from a newspaper stand. "You'd have to be a short midget to be comfortable in a compact," he muttered.

Jimmy Taggert was on his hands and knees, covered in dirt from head to toe. He let the phone ring a dozen times before responding. "Son–of–a–bitch. I'm never gonna get this garden in. My first day off in three weeks and they're already pestering me. What the hell could be wrong this early in the morning?" He grumbled, rising to his feet and walking to the cordless phone. "This better be real important, Max," he said answering the phone.

"Well it's about time. What took you so damn long?"

"Corey?" Jimmy asked.

"That'd be me."

"How did you know I'd be here?"

"I'm an FBI agent. Remember?"

Jimmy smirked. "You called the office and they told you where to find me. Right?"

Corey laughed. "Yep, Max told me to let the phone ring a good long time. Said you'd be outside in the garden. Can't get farmin' out of your blood, huh?"

"Anne was the one with the green thumb. I'm just trying not to kill anything she planted. How have you been?"

"Hanging in there as best as I can. How about you?"

"About the same. Nothing much happens in Darien. You know your life's pretty much in the crapper when you look forward to the tractor pull at the county fair each year. It doesn't get much more lame than that?"

"It could be worse," Corey remarked.

How's that?"

"What if the tractor pull was cancelled this year? Tell me that wouldn't be depressing."

Jimmy shook his head. "Don't even go there. Folks would be popping Prozac like candy if that ever happened." He used a stick to pry the dirt from the bottom of his boots. "So what's going on? I'm guessing you didn't call to check on my crop rotation."

"I'm in town. Just landed in your fair city, as a matter of fact. I was wondering if you wanted to get together for lunch?"

"Sure, that'd be great. I'm assuming you're in town on business…not pleasure."

"I'm heading up the advance detail for the President's visit here this summer. The Canadian Prime Minister and the President will be rededicating the Peace Bridge on its 75th birthday. They'll be signing a brand spanking new trade pact, too. You know our President, he never misses out on the opportunity to have his picture in the paper. Especially when he can tie it to labor and free trade. He's in a tight race. Needs all the votes he can get." Corey pinned the phone between his shoulder and ear while rummaging through his briefcase. "He's a tough son–of–a–bitch. I'll give him that much. I know a guy who served with him in '58. They were SEALS out of Norfolk. Said he was all business, even back then, shoot and ask questions later. Supposedly had quite a knack for taking out sentries. My friend said they did a lot of covert shit in 'Nam before anyone knew we were there. A lot of illegal shit. You know the story…advisors attached to the American Embassy…full diplomatic immunity. A license to kill."

"I never heard that before," Jimmy said.

"He did some nasty shit over there. It's not the kind of thing that helps win elections. He keeps a lid on it…keeps it buried. Buried real deep. He's a good guy, can shoot the shit with the best of 'em. You'd like him. He's a lot like you and me."

"I can't imagine a president being anything like me," Jimmy replied.

"Well, why don't you see for yourself? I'll put you on the invitation list as my guest. You can take part in the ceremony on the bridge. You even get to shake his hand. I'll mark you down unless you've got a better offer."

Jimmy laughed. "Count me in. I usually spend the Fourth on patrol all day and night trying to keep kids from blowing their fingers off."

"It's a deal. Just make sure you shine those shit–kickers of yours. Wouldn't want you showing up looking like the hayseed you are. So what do you say? Can you tear yourself away from the garden for an hour or two?"

"I suppose. Where do you want to go?"

"It's your city. You tell me. Can you meet me on the job site in an hour? It's at the base of the bridge. Just before the tolls. You can't miss it."

"You got it. I'll be there at 11:00. You buying?"

Corey laughed out loud. "Don't worry, I'll pick up the tab, you cheap son–of–a–bitch."

"Cheap has nothing to do with it. I know how much you Feds make. You can afford to pop for lunch once in awhile. I'll see you in few hours."

"How's Ryan working out?"

Tom Kauffman leaned against a railing overlooking the Niagara River and stuffed a wad of chewing tobacco in his mouth, stretching his cheek into a rounded mound of flesh. "He's a worker, boss. Barely takes a break. You ask him to go up top or underwater and you don't hear a peep out of him. He works like a dog out there. I wish more of the crew worked as hard. We'd be a month ahead of schedule if they did."

Sean Mahoney lifted his hardhat up and scratched his bristly hair. "How's he getting along with the crew?"

"He keeps to himself mostly. Doesn't eat with them. Brings his lunch religiously. Totes that silver thermos of his wherever he goes. He's quiet, but you get sense that his wheels are always turning. Seems pretty smart, maybe too smart for this line of work. I don't know, Sean. There's something odd about the guy. I can't quite place my finger on it, but something's a bit off." Kauffman picked up a handful of crushed stone and pitched it into the water. He looked over his shoulder, toward the bridge, watching Ryan/Baker weld a fitting closed. "Then again maybe it's nothing. I've been in this business for close to twenty years and ninety–nine percent of the guys I've come across are cut from the same cloth. You know the type, a little frayed at the edges. This cat's different." He leaned further over the railing and spit a slimy brownish drool onto the weathered rocks.

"All I care about is if he's getting the job done. Do me a favor. Tell Ryan to stop in the office during lunch. I need to finish up his paperwork," Mahoney said.

"You got it," Kauffman replied, using his sleeve to wipe the drool from his lips.

Corey stood on the Peace Bridge and looked down at the Niagara. Ferocious currents whipped the ice–cold water into a vicious frenzy, sending waves crashing into the jagged shoreline. "Man! Look at that current. Looks like four to five foot waves out there…maybe six. You take a dive into those rapids and you die in a New York minute. That white–water would batter you up against the piers and rip you to pieces. I've white–watered on the Colorado, and it wasn't as bad." He stuffed the toe of his shoe between the bridge's railings and studied the span from one end to the other. "We'll need to seal the bridge on both ends and shut down the waterway. I don't want any boats coming within a half–mile of here. Set up a meeting with the Canadian authorities. We're taking the lead. This isn't going to be a picnic. The bridge is wide open." He pointed across the river to the distant shore. "There must be a dozen buildings with clean shooting lines. We'll need each of them searched and sealed. I'm guessing we'll need a half–dozen dogs to sniff for explosives. Standard operating procedure on this one, manhole covers and mailboxes welded shut."

Agent Mackey scribbled down notes as Corey spoke, glancing up and nodding every so often, trying hard to look like he knew what he was doing.

"I want a report from the Canadians on recent terrorist activities. Tell them that we need to tighten up things on the border, starting now."

Mackey flipped a page on his note pad and continued writing. A cool, damp wind caught his tie, wrapping it around his neck. "What about air space?"

"Secret Service will handle that. They'll have it sealed so tight that even seagulls won't be able to get within a mile of the bridge. The news stations won't like it...they never do. They like to get their copters nice and close for some tight shots." Corey scanned the length of the bridge again. "What do you think, Agent Mackey? We miss anything?"

Mackey studied the bridge and both shores before responding. He shook his head timidly, not quite sure if he was being tested. "Can't think of anything. Seems like we got it all," he said nervously.

Corey smiled. "Yeah. I'd say so. Let's go meet with Mahoney. The President wants the work crew on the bridge for the ceremony...hardhats and all. He's looking for an early endorsement from the unions. We'll have to run background checks on all of them."

Baker laid his acetylene torch on the girder and pushed the jet–black goggles up over his eyes, letting them rest on a red baseball cap. He held a hand in front of his face while his deep–blue eyes adjusted to the bright sunlight.

"Yo, Ryan!"

Baker turned and looked down, finding Tom Kauffman standing with his back to the Canadian shore. "Yeah."

"The boss wants to see you in the trailer. He needs to get your paperwork done."

Baker offered a faint wave and nodded. "I'm on my way."

Jimmy swung his pickup truck into the parking lot adjacent to the Peace Bridge Plaza at the same time that Baker was climbing down from the bridge's overhead supports. The brisk wind wrapped itself around his wiry body, leaving his face wind–burned and chapped.

"Hey, Taggert! Over here," Corey yelled from the trailer window.

Jimmy waved.

Baker reached the last of the bridge's massive supports and jumped, landing with a thud onto the decking.

"We'll run checks on your men and get back to you," Corey said to Sean Mahoney.

"You can scratch Larry Mehan from the list of names I sent to you last week," Mahoney replied.

"How's that?"

"He drove his car into the river last Friday night. Had *way* too much to drink. They fished his body out of the rapids below the falls a few days later. His face looked as though it'd gone through a meat grinder. Police said he had more alcohol than blood in his body."

Corey shook his head. "Poor bastard. Did he have any kids?"

"No kids…he wasn't married. All he had in this world was a mangy mutt named Lucky."

Corey shoved a pile of papers in his briefcase. "So I've got everything. Right?"

"Not quite. I've got to get you the paperwork on the man that took Mehan's place. He'll be here in a few minutes, if you want to wait. I can have him fill it out and give it to you in person."

Jimmy knocked and opened the door.

Baker stepped over the concrete barrier at the edge of the bridge and headed toward the trailer, taking time to smoke a cigarette along the way.

"Well look what the cat dragged in," Jimmy remarked, sporting a huge grin.

Corey smiled and walked to the door. "Good to see you, Taggert," he said, hugging him tightly. "Good to see you!"

"You're looking good," Jimmy commented. "Dropped a few pounds, huh?"

Corey sucked in his gut and rubbed it with his hand. "I sneak in a workout every now and again." He turned toward Agent Mackey.

"You mind sticking around and waiting for the info on the new guy while the Sheriff and I head to lunch?"

Mackey nodded. "Sure, no problem. Take your time. I'll grab something from the hotdog stand we passed on the way in here."

"Good enough." Corey draped his arm around Jimmy's neck and exited the trailer. "So where are we going to eat?"

"I was gonna take you to this greasy spoon, but with you looking so buff, I don't know."

"I don't care where we eat just as long as the waitresses are hot and they're wearing skimpy, tight–fitting uniforms. Preferably see–through!"

Baker turned the corner just as Taggert and Corey reached the parking lot.

Jimmy sighed. "Cool your jets, skipper! You don't look *that* good! They're in their twenties…*early* twenties! You've got a snowball's chance in——" He glanced back over his shoulder as he stepped into the cab, catching a glimpse of Baker entering the trailer. The hairs on the back of his neck stood on end and a chill ran down his spine. A sinking feeling settled in the pit of his stomach.

"What's the matter? You look like you've seen a ghost," Corey asked.

Taggert ran his fingers through his hair and shook his head. "If I didn't know better, I swear the guy who just entered the trailer was Baker." He forced a smile. "I thought I got him out of my head but I guess I still have a way to go, huh?"

"Don't worry about it. You're not crazy. It happens to me all the time. Sometimes you run into people that remind you of someone else. I remember running into this dude in San Francisco last year. He was the spitting image of this guy I busted in Atlanta a month earlier. Believe me, I did a double take. Even called Fulton to make sure he was still doing time." Corey offered a comforting smile. "You've been through a lot. Take it from me. Baker's going to be in your head for a while longer. He'll pop out at you when you least expect it. But one day he'll be gone and won't come back. He's dead…blown to pieces. That'll never change."

Jimmy slid sunglasses over his eyes and cranked the engine. He slipped his truck into drive and pulled out of the parking lot, staring at the trailer in the rearview mirror. "The greasy spoon it is…if you promise that you'll leave the waitresses alone. Don't go embarrassing me in there, I'm friends with the owner," he joked, trying to push away the uneasiness that still lingered in the pit of his stomach.

CHAPTER 19

Baker struggled to steady himself, clutching a drill in one hand and the railing of the underwater scaffolding in the other. Powerful undercurrents drove his body to the corner of the platform, squeezing his ribs against cold steel. His air tank clanged against its shiny metal. A nylon tether–cord was securely fastened to a harness wrapped tightly around his waist and chest, the other end to the bridge. The water was dark, cold, and thick with sediment, allowing just a few feet of visibility. He took a long, thin roll of *Generation X* from a satchel strung to his belt and slid it deep into the freshly drilled hole in the bridge's caisson. A wireless receiver, disguised as a bolt, was carefully fitted into place, leaving the explosive undetectable. He pulled on a rope fixed to a series of pulleys, inching the platform along steel cables to the adjoining caisson. He steadied the drill, using the platform's railing for support, and began boring through the reinforced concrete. The diamond–tipped drill cut easily, spitting chunks of concrete onto the riverbed.

Storm clouds pushed across the darkened sky, quickly choking the failing sunlight. A cold wind pushed hard against Sean Mahoney's back. "It doesn't look good. The wind's really picking up. We'll have six–foot swells soon," he bemoaned.

Tom Kauffman flipped the collar of his coat up and nodded. "Yep, it looks like we've got some real bad–ass thunder–boomers headed our way. They'll pick up steam when they roll across the lake. It'll be nasty as hell on the water. The waves will eat up anybody stupid enough to stay out there."

"That's what I'm afraid of. We'd better break camp for the day. Get the crew in. Tell 'em to tie everything down tight. Real fucking tight. And send someone down to get Ryan. The river's already starting to rock. He'll be tossed around like a rag–doll down there."

Kauffman zipped his coat up. A cold, wet mist slapped his face. "I'll send Eddie O' down," he said. "That fat bastard's been dragging his ass all morning."

Edward O'Neil stuffed his large, flabby body into the skin–tight wet suit and reluctantly climbed into the river. He glanced up at the blackened sky and muttered a half–dozen expletives before submerging below the rolling waves. The coldness of the water quickly penetrated the insulated suit, taking his breath away. He followed the guidewire down, inching his way toward the platform where Baker worked. The light on his helmet barely cut through the murky water, illuminating just a few feet ahead of his outstretched arms. He descended more than thirty feet before gaining his first sight of Baker's light. As he grew closer he noticed his crewmate setting the plastic explosive deep into the caisson. He stopped, floating several yards above the platform. He watched curiously as Baker stuffed wires into the tube and worked the receiver neatly over the hole.

What the fuck is Ryan doing? He asked himself.

Suddenly, Baker caught a glimpse of O'Neil's light and turned sharply, his lifeless eyes pierced the darkness. He darted from the platform a split–second later.

O'Neil turned and scurried away, using the rope to guide him to the surface. The undercurrents pulled against his fat body. His heart pumped wildly, thumping hard against his chest as adrenaline flooded his veins. Streams of bubbles, churning from his mouth-piece, rushed silently to the surface.

Baker hunted him. He glided through the water like a shark, quickly gaining on his prey.

The surface was in sight. O'Neil left the comfort of the rope and stretched for the light. The work crew was too busy rushing off the bridge to notice his hand rise above the water, desperately groping for something to grasp. Long spidery bolts of lightening flashed across a menacing sky. Thunder rumbled below the clouds. Hail poured down, ricocheting off their helmets in a deafening rush.

Baker grabbed firmly on O'Neil's ankle, pulling him back under. He moved quickly, ripping the air hose from his tank with one hand while wrapping the tether–cord through his belt with the other, anchoring him firmly to the bottom.

O'Neil struggled frantically, quickly expending his remaining air. His eyes, fraught with terror, begged for mercy.

Baker offered none. He swam dispassionately alongside him. He kept just out of reach of the Irishman's flailing arms, waiting patiently for the thrashing to cease as his lungs filled with water, before dragging his limp body back to the bottom of the river. He reattached the air hose to the oxygen tank before feeding the body to the relentless undertow. It quickly disappeared into the shadows, leaving Baker all alone on the river's floor.

The platform, battered by four–foot waves, broke to the stormy surface in a rush. It rolled on the turbulent river, pitching violently from side–to–side. Its steel cables strained against the storm's fury. Baker stood at one end with his back braced against the corner. Sheets of rain pelted his face, tearing into his skin. Kauffman stood alone at the edge of the bridge. A bright yellow slicker hid most of his face.

Baker held his hand in front of his eyes. "Shit. I should have stayed down. It's a fucking nightmare up here," he yelled into the howling wind.

"Hey, Ryan. Where the fuck's O'Neil?" Kauffman asked.

"How the hell would I know? I've been working underwater all morning," Baker answered.

"I sent him down to get you ten minutes ago."

Baker shook his head. "I never saw him!"

Kauffman snatched a walkie–talkie from his belt. "Sean, it's me. O'Neil's missing! He went under and never came up. You'd better get hold of the Coast Guard," he shouted above the din.

* * *

The better part of a day passed before the storm let up and the Coast Guard was able to search the river. Two more days would come and go before Edward O'Neil's bloated body washed up on shore more than three miles downstream. Fish had picked over most of his flesh, birds and small rodents claimed what little remained.

CHAPTER 20

The Presidential motorcade exited the interstate at Porter Avenue. It approached the Peace Bridge at the same time that the Prime Minister's limousine turned onto the bridge from the Canadian side of the Niagara River. The freshly painted bridge glistened in the late afternoon sun. Mahoney's crew, dressed in work clothes, complete with hardhats and steel–toed boots, stood proudly to the side. Baker stood alone in the back row, leaning against the shiny steel railing. His hardhat was pulled tight to his eyebrows, leaving a shadow covering much of his face. A month–old goatee and pair of thick, black–rimmed sunglasses served as his only disguise. The bridge's massive span was lined with scores of people and dignitaries, each rising up on their toes to catch a first glimpse of the President.

Mitchell Corey rode in the lead car, two ahead of the limousine carrying President Andrews. Sheriff Taggert sat next to him. His uniform was neatly creased and his shoes were brightly polished.

Security was tight. Secret Service agents dotted the surrounding landscape, from rooftops to the water's edge. A Coast Guard helicopter was on standby in a nearby offshore hanger. Two heavily armed Coast Guard cutters blockaded the river a mile downstream. Traffic had long since been diverted from the roadways, leaving the motorcade an eerily deserted route to follow.

Canadian Prime Minister Pierre Moustaeau left the safety of the limousine and stepped out onto the hot concrete. The short, stocky politician waddled to the center of the bridge and stepped up on the brightly decorated dais. He combed his thinning hair with his fingers, pushing it across his sunburned forehead. Canadian and US flags fluttered in the gentle breeze and seagulls circled the bridge, casting long shadows on its refurbished deck. He waved heartily to the cheering crowd, soaking up as much of the limelight as he could before the American leader arrived.

Moments later, the President's limousine came to a halt. A dozen secret service agents exited the motorcade, joining another dozen already on the bridge.

Agent Corey studied the horizon and spoke into a microphone fixed to his watch before opening the President's door and helping him to his feet. Jimmy stood at his side, feeling more out of place than he could ever remember. President John Andrews rose, buttoned his dark blue suitcoat, and waved to the exuberant crowd. The handsome president was tall, with broad shoulders and an athletic build. His deep blue eyes squinted in the falling sun.

Baker leaned forward, straining for a better view. His cold eyes narrowed as they followed Corey guiding the President through the thick crowd. A slow, haunting smile rose on his face as he caught a glimpse of Taggert trailing a few feet behind. "Well…well…well, look what the cat dragged in. Darien's finest. Welcome to the party, Sheriff," he whispered. He glanced at his watch and snickered. "Perfect. Absolutely perfect. Who says you can't kill two birds with one stone? Nothing like one stop shopping."

President Andrews and Prime Minister Moustaeau shook hands at the center of the bridge amid an explosion of flash bulbs and applause.

The choreographed crowd rose to its feet, holding signs and waving small American and Canadian flags. A marching band played the Canadian National Anthem followed by "The Star Spangled Banner." Fireworks rocketed high into the turquoise sky as the last note played. High school cheerleaders, pom–poms in hand, paraded in front of the two leaders. The Prime Minister sank his dark, beady eyes deep into their skin–tight uniforms and salivated. The President mustered just enough strength to turn and look away.

While everyone's attention was riveted on the President, Baker bent forward and slid the heel of his boot to the side, exposing a small compartment crammed with two transmitters. He attached a wire that ran under his shirt to one of the transmitters and slid it into a pocket sewn on the inside of his shirt. He held the other transmitter firmly in the palm of his hand and stepped forward toward the President, forcing his way through the tightly packed crowd. He was ten yards from President Andrews when the first secret service agent noticed him and spoke into his microphone. Seconds later, Baker felt a hand close tightly around his upper arm.

"Excuse me, sir. May I see your ID?" the stone–faced agent demanded.

Baker turned and smiled. "Why don't you go fuck yourself," he said calmly.

The agent dug deeper into Baker's arm and pulled while speaking into his microphone. "This is Smith. We've got a situation in the southeast sector."

"Southeast sector, huh? I've always had a terrible sense of direction. I couldn't tell you if we were facing north or south. If it wasn't for the sun, I wouldn't know east from west either. You secret service guys always impressed me with that shit. It must be in your blood. Genetic, I'm guessing. But enough small talk. You've got a lot more than a *situation* here. You best get a whole lot of back up, spanky. The party's just beginning."

"Been dipping into the sauce. Haven't you, pal?" Agent Smith said dismissively, reaching for his cuffs. A half–dozen agents poured through the crowd, quickly surrounding Baker.

"Ahh, the calvary has arrived. Not too shabby of a response time either. Corey's done a good job," Baker commented. He pulled away just the agent was about to cuff his hands behind his back.

The other agents moved decisively.

Baker stepped back and held the hand with the transmitter high over his head. "BACK UP! EVERYONE STEP BACK!"

Corey turned sharply toward the commotion and barked an order into the microphone. A split–second later, a dozen agents, with weapons drawn, surrounded the President and rushed him to the limousine. Corey raced towards Baker. Taggert followed. The Canadian Prime Minister scrambled for his car as spectators sprinted wildly in all directions.

Agents flooded the bridge, trying futilely to calm the panicked crowd.

"The fucking bridge is wired. Take a step toward me and I'll light it up!" Baker yelled over the din.

Six agents trained their weapons on Baker.

"DROP IT! DROP WHAT YOU'RE HOLDING AND PLACE YOUR HANDS BEHIND YOUR HEAD! DO IT NOW!" Agent Smith ordered. His heart raced and muscles tensed.

Baker turned his head slightly, catching a glimpse of the President's limousine speeding off the bridge, and calmly pressed the first of three red buttons.

The American side of the bridge blew, sending a fifteen–foot wide section of the road tumbling into the Niagara. The driver locked the brakes but couldn't stop the limousine in time. It skidded to a halt with its front–end teetering on the edge, threatening to slide over the brink. The President was thrown against the door. His head crashed against the bulletproof glass. Agents were frantic. They tried desperately to keep the car level as they extricated the dazed President. Debris slid from under the car, leaving the limousine with a fleeting foothold. Andrews' upper torso was halfway through the door.

Suddenly the car pitched. It lurched sharply forward, leaving its back tires floating above the pavement. Sparks flew as the metal undercarriage scraped against the broken concrete. An agent grabbed the President's arm and pulled as another pushed from the backseat. His hand was wet with sweat. He could feel his grip slipping.

Just as the car seemed to gain its balance, a huge wedge of concrete tore away from the bridge, dragging the limo down with it. The agent lost his grip and the President fell. The jagged concrete cut into his side as he slid over the edge. He flailed his arms frantically, aimlessly groping for a slice of the bridge, catching hold of a rusted girder at the last possible second. He dangled perilously at the crumbling edge, watching helplessly as the shiny, new limousine, with three agents trapped inside, crashed into the water and was quickly swept away. Another agent rushed to the President's rescue, clutching his hand. They slowly pulled him to the safety of the deck.

Baker's lips curled into a sadistic smile. "Now there's something you don't see everyday," he quipped. He watched a crowd of spectators racing toward the opposite end of the bridge and waited until they were only yards from leaving the span before pressing the second button.

A split–second later, another explosion rocked the bridge. Trestles and girders snapped like twigs, plunging the Canadian side of the structure into the river, taking dozens of people with it. Parents, with children wrapped tightly in their arms, fell and were swallowed by the swirling water. Their haunting screams echoed in the gorge. Most died on impact, some were buried by falling debris. A few were swept down river only to be crushed under the tremendous weight of the Falls.

The explosion left the middle of the span a concrete and steel island, trapping those that remained. The terrified hostages huddled together. They clutched the railing in the center of the bridge. Some screamed. Some cried. Some went into shock. All of them prayed.

"London Bridge is falling down…falling down…falling down," Baker sang. "I've got one button left and it takes out what we're standing on. If I press down on the plunger the bridge blows and everyone dies…including the fucking President," he yelled. "Now tell your men to toss their heaters over the rail and step back. You place yours on the ground and kick it over here. Do it now!"

"What do you want?" Smith asked, keeping his pistol trained on Baker. There was a slight panic in his voice.

"I'll talk to Corey about that. You've got three seconds, Mr. Smith. I'll send us all to hell if your men don't feed their pistols to the river."

"Do as he says," Corey said, breaking through the ring of secret service agents surrounding Baker. "Lose your weapons."

Baker took his hat off and smiled. "You always were smarter than you looked, Corey," he teased. "Surprised to see me?"

Corey didn't respond. An icy stare was all he offered.

"And look who's standing behind you. Step up, Sheriff. Don't be shy. Let me get a good look at you."

Taggert stepped forward, alongside of Corey.

"You're looking good, Jimmy. *Real* good! I like the uniform. The old lady must have spent all morning pressing it."

Jimmy's eyes narrowed. He clenched his fists. Corey placed a hand on his shoulder. "Take it easy, man. Don't let him fuck with you," he whispered.

"Oh, that's right. There is no Mrs. Taggert. You're holding your own now. It completely slipped my mind. By the way, the red geraniums you've planted at her grave look great. I'm sure she'd approve. I wouldn't have picked you as the gardening type, though. You look more like a field and stream kinda guy. Bet you got a whole closet full of flannel shirts."

"What do you want?" Corey interrupted in a voice that hummed with anger.

"I'll get to that in a moment." Baker leaned forward and picked up agent Smith's pistol. "I know what you're thinking. You're wondering if one of the sharpshooters you've got sitting on top of those buildings across the river can take me out before my finger pushes the button. Aren't you? Well, tell 'em to keep their fingers off the trigger because I've got another transmitter wired to an electrode that's taped to my chest. If my heart stops beating the bridge comes down. And don't go thinking you can shoot the transmitter out of my hand and rush me. It's sending a signal to the detonator as we speak. If the signal's interrupted the bridge crumbles. I know how you motherfuckers think. I've thought of everything. Believe me." He looked at the piles of rubble at the ends of the bridge. "I used good old–fashioned dynamite on the first two explosions. I saved the good stuff for the grand finale. You know what a few bars of *Generation X* are capable of doing. There won't be anything left standing."

Corey spoke into his microphone. "Tell everyone to holster their weapons," he said reluctantly. Thin lines of sweat rolled down his forehead. A sinking feeling settled in the pit of his stomach.

"Good. Now I'd like a conversation with the Prime Minister and President. Would you be kind enough to bring them to me?"

"You know I can't do that."

Baker pointed the gun at Agent Smith and calmly pulled the trigger.

Smith clutched his chest and collapsed to the ground, gasping for air. Blood quickly colored his shirt and suit, pouring onto the concrete. Corey rushed to his aid but there was nothing he could do to stop the loss of blood. He watched helplessly as the agent bled to death.

"You son–of–a–bitch! He had a wife and two kids. Why did you kill him?" Corey screamed, rising to his feet.

"You're an FBI agent. You should know. I'm setting the ground rules. That's the first thing you need to establish in a hostage situation. Can't have negotiations without ground rules, now can we, agent man? That's what they teach you at the academy. Isn't it?"

Corey took his suitcoat off and placed it gently over Smith's head.

"Hand me the extra clips Smith had for this Glock. He won't be needing them anymore. And I'll see the President now," Baker insisted. "Do it or the next one to die will be a civilian…maybe one of those sweet little cheerleaders over there. There's a cute blonde with a tight ass and killer tits that I'm a bit smitten with. I'd much rather shove something other than the barrel of this pistol in that pretty mouth of hers. If you know what I mean," he said, and winked.

Corey stood and stared at Baker for a long moment before whispering into his microphone.

"Now that wasn't so hard. Was it? Agent Smith would be coming home to his wife and kids if you would have just done what I asked. You're just as responsible for his death as I am…maybe more."

"Don't you dare blame it on me, you piece–of–shit! You're awful tough when you're standing with a pistol in your hand. Aren't you? We'll settle this someday you fucking weasel. Just you and me," Corey snapped.

"You'll have to stand in line. I think Taggert's ahead of you," Baker said laughing. "It's so easy to press your buttons. Like a puppet on a string, almost as easy as the Sheriff. You're both so friggin' predictable. How many years have you been trying to catch me now? You haven't even come close. You're pathetic. I bet you have trouble finding your dick when you need to take a leak. Or maybe you just wet your pants."

"What is it you want?" President Andrews demanded, pushing past Corey. He struggled to catch his breath. His clothes were torn and bloody. A cut ran up his side, from the bottom of his ribs to his armpit. A three–inch gash ran diagonally across his right cheek. Blood oozed from both wounds.

"My country doesn't negotiate with terrorists," the Canadian Prime Minister added. "You won't get any money from us."

Baker stared at the President with cold, penetrating eyes. "You look like shit. Guess you won't be kissing any babies today, huh? Try not to bleed on me. Okay?" He turned toward Moustaeau and smiled. "I don't want any money from you or your country. Your money's good for shit. The exchange rate sucks. But what can you expect from a country that uses a maple leaf for its national emblem, and can't decide whether to use English or French as its national language? No, Mr. Moustaeau, I'm not interested in your fucking money. But I do need you to convey a message for me. Even a pathetic loser like you should be capable of that much. French or English. Take your pick. It doesn't matter to me."

"I'll not participate or aid you in anyway, sir. You're nothing but a thug!"

Baker laughed out loud. It was a deep, bellowing laugh. The kind that grates at you. "Sure you will. You see that news copter up there? It'll be close enough for a picture in a half–minute or so. I took the liberty of calling them earlier today. Told 'em there might be a kick–ass story. One that can make a reporter's career. Look what the Kennedy assassination did for Dan Rather! He was nothing but a two–bit reporter until he was lucky enough to cover JFK's trip to Dallas. Talk about being in the right place at the right time. That bastard must of had one hell of a horseshoe stuck up his ass that day. Just think, if JFK didn't buy the farm, Rather would still be reporting about the annual pie–eating contest at the county fair in Jerkwater, USA."

"Do you really think I'm going to say something to the press on your behalf? Is that what this is all about? A political statement of some sort?"

"I never mix politics with business. Never," Baker swore.

The copter drew closer, allowing the cameraman to get a clear shot of the bridge.

"Smile…the whole world's watching," Baker announced. "THIS IS CNN." He put the gun to the Prime Minister's head and pulled the trigger. "Ask not what your country can do for you. Ask what you can do for your country," he said laughing.

Moustaeau's body fell over the rail and plunged headfirst into the river. It bobbed on the choppy water and was carried over the Falls a few minutes later. "A picture's worth a thousand words. Wouldn't you agree, Mr. President?"

Andrews lunged for Baker. "YOU GOD DAMN BASTARD," he screamed.

Baker pistol–whipped the President, knocking him to his knees.

Agent Malloy rushed Baker.

Baker quickly shoved the barrel of his gun against the President's forehead. "TAKE ANOTHER STEP AND I'LL FUCKING POP HIM," he yelled. "Better get a leash on your man, Corey. Reel the prick in. Reel him in NOW!"

Corey grabbed Malloy and pushed him back. "Take it easy, Sean. Get a grip."

"Not a smart move, Sean. You've got balls, but no brains. Not a good combination. Especially for someone in your line of work," Baker commented. "I was always fascinated by the fact that you guys say that you'll lay down your life for the President. *Take a bullet for him*, isn't that what you say when you're at the neighborhood pub throwing back a few with your testosterone bloated buddies?" He kept the barrel of the gun butt up against Andrews' forehead. "It's an interesting concept, but I'm not convinced you'd actually do it. Not when push comes to shove."

"I've got him under control. He made a mistake. He's new. Why don't you pull the gun away from the President? You don't want it going off accidentally," Corey said in a calm voice.

The news copter hovered at the edge of the bridge, broadcasting live. Wind from its rotors whipped across the deck. On any other day, the breeze would have seemed comforting.

Jimmy took a pocketknife from his jacket, opened it, and slid it up his sleeve without anyone noticing.

Baker looked at Malloy. "Would you take a bullet for the President, Sean?"

"We don't need to go there. You made your point," Corey pleaded.

Baker glared at Corey. "Shut the fuck up. I'm not talking to you." He turned back toward Malloy. "Well...would you?"

"Yes, I would," Malloy answered, taking a subtle step backwards. "It's my job." There was a noticeable quiver in his voice.

Baker stared at the agent. "Your eyes say no. Let's see just how serious you are. Walk to the edge, climb on top of the railing, and jump."

Malloy looked at him and laughed. It was an uneasy laugh. The kind you make when you're trying to hide your fear. "Yeah, right," he muttered.

"I'm not kidding. Either you jump off the bridge or I bury a bullet in the President's skull. It's your call."

Malloy looked at Corey with desperate eyes.

"Don't do this," President Andrews pleaded. "You don't need—"

Baker drove a knee hard into the President's jaw. "You may be top dog in the beltway but out here you're nothing. So keep your fucking mouth shut. This is my parade. Don't rain on it. Open your mouth again, and I'll drill you."

"What's it going to be, Sean? You or him? It doesn't make a difference to me."

Malloy took several uneasy steps toward the edge of the bridge.

Taggert took a step forward.

Baker turned sharply. "Don't try and be hero today, Taggert. Remember what happened the last time that you tried? Back off."

Corey pulled Taggert back. "Don't. He's holding all the cards right now."

Jimmy glared at Baker and slowly backed off.

"Smart move. And they say you can't teach an old dog new tricks. Seems like you're finally learning, Sheriff." He turned his attention back to Malloy. "You've got ten seconds to climb up on the railing. I won't give you a second more."

Malloy was sweating profusely as he shuffled past his colleagues and climbed on top of the railing. His heart pounded against his chest, his body trembled. The pit of his stomach was a churning mess. His suitcoat fluttered in the swirling wind. He looked down at Baker with eyes begging for mercy.

He found none.

"Jump," Baker ordered.

Malloy hesitated.

Baker thrust the gun barrel against the President's head. "I'll do him right now if you don't."

Malloy swallowed hard, closed his eyes and stepped off the railing, plunging into the water a second later.

"What do you know…he did it," Baker said. "Your men are loyal, Corey. I'll give you that much." He stepped back and let the President rise to his feet.

"What is it you want?" Andrews asked. His voice was coarse and demanding, almost threatening.

"Ten billion dollars."

"You're out of your mind!" Andrews snapped.

"So what's your point? I want ten billion transferred to an account number that I'm going to give Agent Corey in a moment. If the money isn't transferred in thirty minutes then I'll begin killing the hostages. One for each minute you delay. And it will all be seen live on TV. I'll start with the woman and children. They tend to scream a bit more than men. It'll make for better TV. You won't even be able to run for town clerk if you let that happen."

"You'll never get away with this. We'll track you down no matter where you go. You'll find no sanctuary—no haven. You've got to know that," the President asserted.

"That's my problem. Isn't it? The problem you need to work on is getting the money together. You've just wasted thirty seconds. Don't fuck with me. Ask Corey or Taggert what happens if you do."

"Let some of the hostages go. It will be a sign of good faith. It'll help grease the wheels," Corey said.

"It's a sign of good faith that I'm not killing a hostage each minute it takes you bastards to collect the money. I'm giving you the first thirty minutes free. Don't push your luck and don't ask again. Get on the horn and get the cash. And the news copter stays. It's the only thing I'll allow within a mile of the bridge. Tell the Chairman of the Joint Chiefs not to bother dispatching Special Forces. This party will be over long before they get here." Baker handed Corey a folded piece of paper. "You give them this account number. Tell them they have thirty minutes. Tell them to keep the bridge clear. Then I want you to inform them that there won't be any other calls. They can watch CNN for updates just like the rest of the world. After you make the call, you and your men sit down on the pavement with your legs crossed…the President included. You do what I ask or the Vice President will be sleeping in the White House tonight."

Corey snatched the paper from Baker's hand and dialed his cellphone.

Baker leaned back against the railing and let the sun warm his face.

CHAPTER 21

Corey turned off the cellphone and slid the antenna down. "They're working on the transfer. You should have the money in a few minutes."

Baker lifted his sunglasses up over his eyes and glanced at his watch. "They've got three minutes. Not a second more," he grunted, sliding the sunglasses back down. His outstretched arms rested comfortably on the railing.

Jimmy leaned close to Corey and whispered. "He's going to light this bridge up whether you give him the money or not. You know that. Don't you?"

Corey nodded. "Yeah, I know. Look at the smug look on that cocksucker's face. He's got us by the balls and he knows it. I'm all out of ideas, man. How about you?"

Jimmy turned his head ever so slightly to steal a glimpse of Baker. "Can you get everyone off the bridge in four minutes?" he asked after a lengthy pause.

Corey studied the hostages. They were scattered across the bridge. "It'd be a tight fit but I think we'd get everyone in the Coast Guard copter." He paused and glanced at the hostages again. "Yeah, I'd get 'em to safety. What's on your mind?"

"Tell your marksmen to shoot the gun from his hand when I give the signal. I'll take care of Baker and the transmitter. It'll take four minutes to reach the Falls once we hit the water. I can stop him from detonating the charge up to that point. All bets are off after that. He'll be crushed by the water once he goes over the brink. The charge will be ignited when the bastard's heart stops."

Corey raised an eyebrow. "Once *we* hit the water?"

Jimmy looked him in the eye. "I've got to go into the water with him. He'll detonate the charge if I don't. There's no other way."

"That means you go over the Falls, too."

Taggert offered a slight nod and looked away. "You can't always have a happy ending."

There was an uneasy pause. He stared at the hostages huddled at the center of the bridge. A young mother cradled her sobbing infant, trying in vain to comfort him. An elderly woman knelt with her face buried in her hands and prayed out loud. A cheerleader sat with her back against the railing and legs drawn tight to her chest, trembling from head to toe. She mumbled incoherently while rocking her head back and forth. President Andrews sat in the middle of a pack of secret service agents, engulfed by an overwhelming sense of helplessness.

"I'm not going to let them die. That bastard's killed too many people already. I won't let him win. Not again. Not this time." He looked at Baker. "He's overconfident. You can hear it in his voice. See it in his walk. He won't be expecting anything. I can take the prick…I can take him right to hell."

Corey rubbed his chin with his forefinger and thumb. "How do you think he's planning on getting off the bridge?"

"The smart money's on the news copter. He'll take a hostage with him for insurance. The President offers the best policy. Once he's off the bridge, the rest of the hostages aren't of any value to him. He'll light it up from the air. It's the perfect distraction. You'll have women and children thrashing in the water, fighting for their lives. The Coast Guard will have to turn their attention and resources to a search and rescue operation. It'll tie 'em up. Keep them from going after the President. We've got to get to him before he gets off the bridge or the game's over."

Corey put his hand on Taggert's shoulder. "You're a good man, Jimmy…a damn good man. But this is my gig. He crashed *my* party. I'll take the trash out," he said.

Jimmy shook his head. "You're needed here. It's going to be a real mess when this goes down. It's your job to see that the President gets out of here in one piece. You put your hand on the Bible and took an oath. Remember?"

Corey hesitated, running his fingers through his hair. "Okay. You've got the ball," he agreed grudgingly.

Taggert nodded. "Tell Max to look after Nattie for me. See that she's comfortable. Will you?"

"You got it. I'll see to it personally."

Jimmy forced a smile. "We better get started. We're running out of time. Tell your man to take his shot when I adjust my hat. Then get that bird up here. Get it up here fast. The clock will start running when we hit the water. The wind's out of the north today. The current's always stronger when that happens. The water will be pushing 20 knots…maybe more. You might not even have four minutes." He stood up, brushed off his pants and walked slowly towards Baker.

Corey spoke quietly into his microphone.

"It turned out to be a nice day after all. Wouldn't you say, Sheriff?"

"It was you I saw at the bridge the day I met Corey for lunch. You used Ryan's birth certificate to get a fake ID for the job with the work crew. Didn't you?"

"Correct–a–mundo! Always said you were as sharp as a tack. By the way, how is Nattie? Is that social security guzzling cow still alive? Or is the old bat pushing up daises alongside her husband's rotting corpse?"

"Why are you here? You could blow the bridge anywhere within a mile of this place. Why complicate things? Why take the risk?" Jimmy probed.

"Now where would the fun be in that?" Baker shook his head and smirked. "No, I like it up close and personal. Flipping a switch from a mile away seems too sterile. Too clinical. If you're going to kill someone you should have the decency to do it to their face. That's my motto…my creed. McVeigh and Kaczynski were fucking cowards. They got no balls. It makes you appreciate guys like Bundy and Dalmer. They took matters into their own hands. Weren't afraid to get 'em dirty, or in their case…bloody." He scratched his nose with the barrel of the gun. "Now please move. You're standing in my sun. Why don't you go bother Corey?"

"That's what this is all about. Isn't it? *Your* moment in the sun. *Your* fifteen minutes of fame." Taggert inched closer. He let the pocketknife that was tucked under his sleeve slide down until the blade rested on the edge of his palm.

The smile left Baker's face. He wiped the sweat off his forehead with the back of his hand. "Don't try and analyze me. You don't know anything about me. Probably read the friggin' FBI profile of me and think you're a fucking expert. You are one irritating son–of–a–bitch. Have been from the moment I saw you. You've got a real knack for it. It comes natural to you. Now why don't you mosey on over to the other side of the bridge and get the fuck out of my sight before I cap your sorry ass right now?"

Jimmy took another step forward and pressed Baker. He let the knife drop into his hand. "Getting a little *hot* under the collar. Aren't you? Not quite as cool as you let on. Whose buttons are easy to press now? Just like a puppet on a string. Isn't that what you said a few minutes ago?"

Baker stood up straight and pointed the pistol at Taggert. The veins in his neck bulged. His face turned red. "I was planning on killing you last but I'm not a very patient man. It's one of my few flaws. If the money's not transferred in a sixty seconds *you* buy the farm...you're the sacrificial lamb." He thrust the barrel of the gun deep into the sheriff's ribs.

Jimmy laughed. "Do you think they're really going to let you off this bridge? Are you that delusional? Look around. You've got sharpshooters coming out your ass!" He shook his head. "You're going down. The problem is that you're too full of yourself to see it. You made the same mistake at Attica. Remember? Thought you had it all figured out...the perfect escape. You walked away, but what about the rest of your crew? Slater and Robinson were cut to pieces and the only thing left of your buddy Peterson was his lower jaw. They found it embedded in a floorboard. Right where you left him to die."

Baker drew a deep breath and stared at Taggert for a long moment before pulling the gun from his gut. "You had me going there for a second, Sheriff. Yeah, you sure as hell did. I have to give it to you...you got under my skin for a second. You're an annoying motherfucker...that's for sure. But you did make it interesting. Believe it or not, I'm going to miss you. I really am." He looked down at his watch and grinned. "Time's up."

He cocked the hammer on his pistol at the same time Jimmy reached for his hat.

A single shot echoed in the canyon.

CHAPTER 22

The gun exploded from Baker's hand, landing on the concrete with his forefinger and thumb still wrapped around its pearl–colored handle.

Jimmy pounced, sticking the knife deep into Baker's eye while planting his shoulder into his chest and lifting him, headfirst, over the steel railing.

Baker reeled with pain. The transmitter flew from his hand as he groped blindly for the knife. Blood gushed from his eye and hand. His ear–piercing scream resonated in the gorge as he fell.

Taggert crashed into the water with such force that it felt as though every inch of his skin had been peeled from his body. Baker plunged into the river a split–second later, narrowly missing him. They bobbed like corks on the rough water as they were sucked towards the Falls.

"Get the fucking copter up here now!" Corey yelled. He raised his arm over his head and made a swirling motion. "Come on! Come on! Move it!"

Secret service agents pulled the President to his feet. Hostages looked to them for direction.

The Coast Guard helicopter was in the air a half–minute later racing towards the bridge. Two Coast Guard cutters sliced through the water with their throttles opened full. The news copter hovered close–by. Its cameraman hung from an open door.

Baker screamed as he pulled the knife from his eye. He swung it wildly, slicing across the Sheriff's neck and shoulder. He adjusted his grip and drew back the knife for a second attack.

Jimmy blocked his arm at the last possible second.

Baker grunted and came at him again.

Huge swells tossed the two men back and forth.

The Coast Guard helicopter landed on the bridge. The wind from its huge rotors ripped across the deck, turning the bridge into a wind tunnel.

"WE'VE GOT TO GET YOU OUT OF HERE!" Corey yelled above the roar of the rotors.

President Andrews pulled free of Corey's grip and turned away. "NO. THE HOSTAGES GO FIRST. GET THEM OFF THE BRIDGE," he yelled.

Corey grabbed the President again. "I HAVE ORDERS, MR. PRESIDENT…YOU GO FIRST!"

Andrews turned sharply. "YOUR ORDERS HAVE JUST BEEN CHANGED. GET THE CIVILIANS OFF THIS BRIDGE. GET THEM ON THE COPTER. DO IT NOW!"

Corey looked at him and glanced back at the hostages. "YOU HEARD THE PRESIDENT. GET THE CIVILIANS LOADED ON THE CHOPPER. GET THEM LOADED NOW!" He turned to Andrews. "Orders or no orders, you're getting you on that bird. You can fire me later if you want."

Baker raised the knife over his head and thrust it at Taggert. "You're a fucking corpse. I'm going to slice you to pieces," he shouted. Half his face was covered in blood. His other hand was little more than a bloody stump.

Jimmy grabbed Baker's wrist and pushed with all he had, but the wound to his shoulder had weakened him. He was slowly losing the battle. The knife inched closer to his neck. He could feel his nemesis' breath on his face. "We're both going to die, asshole," he groaned.

A depraved smile crept up on Baker's face. "But I'll have the pleasure of killing you."

Jimmy could feel the edge of the blade cutting into his neck.

Corey and the President loaded the last of the hostages into the belly of the Coast Guard helicopter.

"You're next, Mr. President," Corey said.

Andrews stepped up into the copter and offered his hand. "Come on, let's get out of here."

Corey shook his head. "I took an oath a long time ago. I can't leave a man behind." He turned to the pilot. "Toss me the pistol that's strapped to your waist and get out of here."

He stuffed the gun in his pants and slid the door closed. "GET THAT NEWS COPTER DOWN HERE. TELL IT TO LAND ON THE DECK OR YOU'LL SHOOT IT DOWN," he yelled into his microphone as he raced across the bridge.

He glanced at his watch and shook his head. "Not enough time."

* * *

The roar of the Falls was deafening. It was louder than a thousand trains. Taggert could feel its cool mist on his face. He struggled to stay afloat in the churning whitewater while desperately fighting off Baker's vicious attacks. Out of the corner of his eye he saw the Coast Guard chopper lift off the bridge and rush towards the safety of the shore.

Atta boy, Corey, he thought.

* * *

As Corey was climbing into the news copter he felt a hand on his shoulder. "I thought you could use an extra pair of hands. I took the same oath you did. I can't leave a man behind, either," President Andrews said.

Corey looked up at the Coast Guard copter speeding away and shook his head. "With all due respect, sir, you're one stubborn son–of–a–bitch."

Andrews smiled. "So I've been told."

Corey climbed into the copter, pulled the President inside, and turned toward the pilot. "Get this bird in the air. You've got 30 seconds to make it to the Falls."

* * *

Jimmy's heart raced, thumping wildly against his chest, fueled by the adrenaline that was surging through his veins. The sting of cold steel on his neck sent shivers down his spine. He reached past Baker's outstretched arm and clawed his face. Digging his thumb deep into his bloody eye socket.

Baker screamed and pulled away, buying Taggert a few precious seconds.

Harry Rosen found himself speechless for the first time in his lengthy career. The verbose reporter sat in the back seat of the copter, his mouth wide open, staring in astonishment as the President boarded the copter. *Holy shit! This is it…this is my ticket out of here,* he thought. *I'll be on the national news…sitting right next to Dan Rather.*

Mitchell Corey and President Andrews stood alongside the cameraman, near the open door.

"You getting this?" Rosen mouthed to his cameraman.

Les Warner nodded, grinning from ear to ear. Thoughts of a Pulitzer Prize rattled around his brain.

Corey snatched a long, black video cable from the floor and tied one end to his waist. "Here, wrap this around something solid and tie it tight," he said, tossing the other end to the President. He slid out the door until his foot rested on the helicopter's runner. The wind stung his face. He squinted against the bright sun. "Tell the pilot to step on it. They're almost at the Falls. Tell him to get closer to the water. I've only got about fifty feet of cable," he yelled above the din of the rotors.

Andrews turned to Rosen. "Put that microphone down and lend a hand."

"I'm not missing out on the story of a lifetime," Rosen snapped.

"A man's life is at stake," Andrews pleaded.

Rosen shook his head. "No way! I've got a story to cov—"

The President sent an uppercut crashing into Rosen's chin, sending him sprawling across the chopper. The reporter was out cold before he hit the floor. Andrews turned to Warner. "You've got a chance to make news instead of reporting it. What's is going to be?"

Warner swallowed hard. "What do you need me to do?" he asked, laying his camera on the seat.

* * *

Baker looked back at the helicopter hovering overhead and attacked Jimmy with a renewed sense of urgency. "They're not going to save your ass, Sheriff. No fucking way!" He thrust the knife deep into Jimmy's abdomen and turned it, tearing into his gut. "Ahh, how's that feel?" he snarled. "A whole jar of Tums ain't gonna make that feel better."

Jimmy moaned. Blood trickled from his mouth and his body went limp.

Baker went for the kill. He raised the knife high above his head and sneered. "Nothing quite like the rush of killing a cop. Time to join that whore wife of yours."

CHAPTER 23

Corey grabbed Baker's arm with one hand and wrapped his other around his neck, choking off his air as he dangled precariously from the thin cord tied to the helicopter and steadied by the President. He swayed wildly back and forth as the pilot fought to hold the helicopter in place against strong down drafts.

"Hey, scumbag! I hope you don't mind me dropping in on you." He turned his head, looked back, and yelled. "Tell the pilot to take me up."

Andrews nodded. A moment later the copter climbed, pulling Baker out of the water and dragging him along the river. He fought desperately to free himself from Corey's iron–tight grip.

Jimmy lay, face down, in the savage water. Six–foot swells carried his spent body towards the Falls. He gagged on mouthfuls of blood and water and was quickly losing consciousness.

Out of the corner of his eye, Baker caught sight of the pistol tucked in Corey's belt. He ditched his knife, and spun sharply, grabbing the weapon in one fluid motion and squeezing off three rounds before Corey dropped him. He plunged into the water and was swept over the Falls before he could get off another shot.

The first two rounds whizzed past the helicopter, narrowly missing the President. The third ripped through the floor of the cockpit, killing the pilot instantly.

The helicopter spun out of control. Corey hung on for life, clinging to the cord while being dragged along the Niagara. Plumes of water dug into his face and hands as he skidded along the choppy surface. The copter pitched violently and dropped like a rock, plunging him into the water. He managed to steal a breath before slipping under the waves.

Andrews rushed towards the cockpit. Les Warner locked his arms around a seat post and shut his eyes tight. His long legs dangled out the door. He had the humiliating experience of feeling warm urine run down his pant leg. Rosen, still unconscious, was wedged between the seats and wall, still clutching a microphone in his hand.

Corey fought to make it back to the surface. He gripped the cord and pulled, hand–over–hand, struggling in vain against the force of the water, expending his remaining air in the effort.

The President pulled the pilot from the seat, clutched the stick with both hands and pulled back with all he had. "I hope I can still fly one of these things," he muttered. The gash in his side split open. Searing pain rocketed up his spine as dark red blood surged from the wound. His body shuddered. Rivulets of sweat ran down both sides of his face. Panic quickly set in.

Corey's grip failed as the last of his air left his lungs, dissipating to the surface in clusters of tiny bubbles. Disappearing into the whitecaps.

"COME ON, YOU SON–OF–A–BITCH! Andrews screamed. He pulled back further, ignoring the pain. The helicopter heaved and strained. Rivets popped. The engine groaned and sputtered. Thick black smoke poured from its vents. Its rotors, inches from the water, spun at full speed. "It's now or never," the President grunted, giving one last heave.

The helicopter pitched and turned, slowly righting itself. Andrews punched it, taking the copter up as quickly as he could, wrenching the FBI agent from the watery grave.

Corey gasped for air.

Andrews banked the helicopter hard to the right and sped towards Jimmy.

Taggert was face down in the rapids, less than 100 yards from the Falls. He was barely visible through the thick mist.

"We're only going to get one shot at this," he yelled down to Corey.

Corey expelled the last of the water from his lungs. His eyes narrowed and body tensed. "That's all I'll need!" he barked.

The President lowered the copter and hovered, looking out the side window. He squinted against the setting sun.

Corey latched onto Jimmy and jerked him from the water. The sheriff hung motionless in his outstretched arms. "Got him! Take it up! Hurry!" he yelled. He felt for signs of life as he carried his friend away, a shallow breath, a pulse, the slightest twitch. He found none. "Don't do this, Taggert. Don't die on me. Not when we've come this far. Please, God, don't take him…you don't need to take him now." Tears rolled down his cheeks. He choked on his emotions. The shore seemed a million miles away.

As the President turned the helicopter toward the warm embrace of the shore, the bridge exploded. By the time the billowing ball of fire and smoke cleared, it was gone, leaving the river bare. A single pier jutted through the water, a solitary remnant of the majestic bridge that had spanned the mighty Niagara for seventy–five years.

CHAPTER 24

"How's the old man feeling today?" Corey asked, stepping into the house without knocking. "Still hurting?"

Jimmy looked up from the book he was reading. "Only when I breathe."

Corey smiled. "I thought you were a goner, man. Never seen that much water pumped out of someone's lungs. Bet you took in a quart. Maybe more. You've got more lives than a cat with a horseshoe stuck up its ass and a rabbit's foot wrapped around its neck. You've got to be the luckiest son–of–a–bitch alive." He laid a stack of newspapers and magazines on the oak table that sat in front of the sofa in Jimmy's living room, pushing his coffee mug aside. "You're famous, partner. You're on the cover of the New York Times, USA Today, Buffalo News, and every major paper in the country. They're calling you a real live hero…a super cop. Next thing you know they'll be naming a street after you. I haven't seen anyone get this much press since the OJ trial! Here, see for yourself."

Jimmy shrugged his shoulders. "You're the hero as far as I'm concerned. I only did what anyone else would have, had they'd been in my shoes."

"All I know is that you've got to get healed up before the big ceremony. The President wants to make a big deal of this…wants plenty of press around when he pins that big medal to your chest in the

Rose Garden. He's *way* ahead in the latest polls thanks to you...got the election cinched. The kicker was the photo of him flying the chopper. Folks will be lining up in droves to pull the lever for him this fall. They're talking landslide."

Jimmy cringed. "I don't want *anything* sharp coming *anywhere* near my body," he moaned.

Corey laughed out loud. "Can't say I can blame you. No, sir, can't blame you at all."

"His body turn up?" Jimmy asked, reaching for his coffee.

"No sign of it...not yet anyway. We couldn't send divers in 'til this morning due to the weather. We'll fish him out soon. Probably by tomorrow...the day after at the latest."

Jimmy folded the corner of a page over, closed the book, and laid it on the sofa. "We had two fisherman go over the Falls last year. They got all liquored up and passed out in the boat. It got sucked over the Falls and took them with it...the poor bastards. The first fisherman's body washed up on the shore the next morning. His buddy's didn't show up for five months. It popped up at the base of the Falls one day. Bobbed on the water like a cork. A hell of a sight for the tourists on the Maid of the Mist. I bet they didn't get much sleep that night."

He shook his head. "You can never tell with the Niagara. Baker's body could be wrapped around something on the bottom. Wrapped around something real good. Or it could be wedged in one of the power intakes. There's close to one hundred of 'em. It'll take a while to check all of 'em out. Baker's dead all right. No one's ever gone over the Falls and lived. Not unless they were in a steel barrel, or some other nutty contraption."

"We'll find it. We'll find it even it means sending the Navy dive team in after it," Corey said confidently. He glanced at his watch. "I've got to run, partner. We located his hotel room. I'm going to check it out. See if we come across anymore explosives. You gonna be all right? You need anything before I split?"

"Nope. Got a nurse stopping over. She should be here any minute, as a matter of fact."

Corey raised an eyebrow. "Nurse! Hmm, maybe I can stick around a wee bit longer. She a *head* nurse?"

Jimmy laughed. "You are a dog! That's for sure. But don't waste your time. I don't think she's your type."

Corey was skeptical. "How's that?" he asked.

"Millie Piedmont stands all of five feet and tips the scales at a solid 225. She's as wide as she is tall…real linebacker material. She'd plug a hole with the best of 'em. One hell of a nurse, though. Wouldn't trade her for all the tea in China."

Corey looked at his watch again. "I gotta run," he said, and winked.

Jimmy smiled. "I thought so. I'll see you in the morning. You promised I could kick your ass in checkers again. Remember?"

"I let you win earlier because I felt sorry for you. Tomorrow you're on your own. No more sympathy. No more mercy. Get ready for a good old–fashioned ass–kicking."

"Keep saying it long enough and you might even start believing it."

Corey looked over his shoulder and smiled. "I'll see you in the morning. Get some rest."

"Hey Mitchell," Jimmy said softly.

Corey noticed the change in his tone. "Yeah."

"Thanks for coming back for me. Thanks for saving my life."

Corey turned and looked him in the eye. "You would have done the same for me…in a heartbeat. I'll see you in the morning. I might even bring you a box of doughnuts. Have the checkerboard ready."

"You're still running a fever…101.5. You better get some rest, Sheriff. Too much visiting isn't good for you. You need your sleep," Millie Piedmont lectured, wiping the thermometer with rubbing alcohol before slipping it back in its thin plastic case. She peeled back the bandage that was wrapped around his stomach and shook her head. "You got no business being home. You should have stayed in the hospital for a few days."

"I don't like hospitals…too many sick people there. I'm better off here. I'll be back on my feet in no time. I'm a fast healer…always have been. You'll see."

Mrs. Piedmont raised an eyebrow. "You'd best hope an infection don't set in. You'll be off your feet a good long time if that happens. You're a stubborn old goat, Jimmy Taggert. I'm not about to waste my time trying to get through that thick skull of yours." She carefully laid the bandage back in place. "I'll change this after you get up. You close your bulbs for a spell. I'm going to clean up. It's starting to look and smell like a barn in here. The least your friends could do is pick up after themselves," she said, shaking her head. "I swear, it must be genetic. Mr. Piedmont, God rest his soul, was cut from the same cloth. Wouldn't be caught dead with a dust rag or vacuum in his hand. No, sir. 'Women's work', he used to mutter."

Jimmy smiled. "Why don't you leave things alone and sit for a spell? Catch up on your soap operas."

"You just mind your own beeswax and take a nice long snooze. I'll have dinner ready for you when you wake. You ain't gonna heal on an empty stomach. I can't be coming out here forever you know. Got other folks to tend to…sicker folks. Folks who heed my advice, 'ppreciate my company."

Jimmy surrendered. "Yes, ma'am," he said, closing his eyes. He drifted off to sleep a few minutes later.

Mrs. Piedmont started in the kitchen. She hummed along with a country and western tune that was playing on the radio while cleaning a stack of dishes that cluttered the sink. She never heard the lock turn on the back door, nor the faint footsteps against the tile floor. Hank Williams' voice crackling on the radio would be the last sound to fill her ears.

Baker clasped his bandaged hand over Millie Piedmont's mouth and slit her throat. He pulled the knife hard, cutting her from ear to ear. He held her until she went limp, then eased her large body to the floor before tiptoeing to the living room door. He approached the sofa from behind, holding the knife out in front of him. The floorboards moaned under his weight as he slithered, undetected, across the length of the room. Short shoots of blonde hair slipped out from underneath the black baseball cap that he wore backwards on his head. His face was battered and bruised. His clothes, tattered and torn. A makeshift black leather patch covered what little remained of his eye. He took a deep breath and cleared the last several feet in one fluid motion. His bandaged stub clamped down hard on the Sheriff's mouth as he thrust the edge of the knife against his throat. Jimmy's eyes shot open wide. His body shuddered and heart raced.

Baker stared for a long haunting moment and grinned. His eyes, narrow and dark, were filled with rage. "You know what I'm going to do after I kill you?" he sneered. "I'm going to pay Nattie Ryan a visit. I'm going to kill her just for the fun of it. Nice and slow. Might even fuck the bitch first." He raised the knife high over his head. His grin turned to a scowl and his eyes narrowed. "Looks like I win after—"

A bullet tore through Baker's chest, exploding out his back. He staggered, regained his balance, and came at Jimmy again, screaming. A second bullet took his life. He fell backwards to the floor, still clutching the knife in his hand. A pool of blood colored the floorboards as the last flicker of life faded from his eyes. His last breath was little more than a whimper.

Jimmy looked up to find Max Wakefield standing in his doorway holding a box in one hand and his service revolver in the other. He was white as a ghost and shaking from head to toe.

"Is he…is he…dead?" Max stammered.

"Yeah, Max. This time he's really dead."

Max swallowed hard. "Never killed a man before."

"You did what you had to. You did your job."

Max nodded. An uneasiness settled in the pit of his stomach. His arm dropped to his side, and suddenly his gun felt too heavy to hold.

Taggert, grimacing, pushed himself up off the sofa, tearing his stitches. Blood began to soak through his bandage. "Got to check on Millie," he groaned, ignoring the wrenching pain in his stomach. "She's in the kitchen."

Max shook his head and frowned. "It's too late. There's nothing you can do. She's already dead," he said softly.

Jimmy slumped back down on the sofa and buried his head in his hands. "You better get Corey on the horn. Tell him to call off the search," he said after a long pause.

"I'll get on it right away, Sheriff."

Taggert ran his fingers through his hair and rubbed his eyes. "Best get Richie and the coroner up here, too. There'll be questions that need answering. Reports that need completing."

"You got it. Right after I get hold of Corey," Max answered, grabbing the police radio off his shoulder.

"Not that I'm complaining but just what are you doing here anyway?" Jimmy asked.

"Nattie baked you an apple pie. Said it'd help get you back on your feet. She made me take it over to you tonight while it was still warm. You know how demanding she can be."

Jimmy smiled. "A regular drill sergeant at times. God bless her."

CHAPTER 25

"I'm going to go to Washington for a few days, spend some time with Corey. He's got a log cabin that overlooks the Potomac. Says he knows a secret fishing hole…one where the trout jump onto your hook. Have to beat 'em off with a stick, he says. He doesn't strike me as much of an outdoorsman so I'm a tad bit skeptical. Seems outdoors challenged if you want to know the truth." Jimmy poured more water in the urn filled with red geraniums at his wife's grave. "You'd like Corey. He reminds me a lot of Bobby Ryan. Makes me laugh." A hazy sun climbed over the tree line, warming the crisp morning air.

"I finally got around to planting a white maple in the corner garden. You were always after me to do that. Remember? It looks good. Like it always belonged there. And I know if you were here you'd tell me 'I told you so.' A pair of blue jays already set up shop there. Wish you could see it," he said, wiping a tear from his cheek. He stood, brushing the dirt from his knees. "I'm doing okay now. The days don't go by quite as slow as they used to. Can't say the same for the nights, though. That's when I miss you the most." He cleared the lump in his throat and forced a smile. "I've decided to keep sheriffing a bit longer. Keeps me busy. Keeps me out of trouble."

"Sheriff, it's Max. You there?"

Jimmy squeezed the button on his walkie–talkie. “Yeah, Maximus. What is it?”

“Johnny McCoy took off after the Hatfield twins again, grabbed his shotgun and jumped into his truck.”

“What happened?”

“You’re not gonna believe this,” Max’s voice crackled on the speaker.

“With everything that’s happened this past week, I can’t imagine anything surprising me.”

Max laughed. “The Hatfield twins filled a paperbag full of manure, set it on Johnny’s porch and put a match to it.”

“Don’t tell me he fell for that one.”

“In a *big* way. Stomped the shit out of it…no pun intended.”

“What a dumb–ass,” Jimmy commented.

“It gets worse.”

“How’s that?”

“Seems old Johnny was wearin’ a brand, spanking new pair of work boots. Fresh out of the box. Didn’t have a lick of dirt on ‘em.”

“Well, now he’s got a pair of shit kickers…pun intended,” Jimmy joked.

Max laughed. “I don’t think Johnny found it all that funny.”

“I don’t suppose he would. He never did have much of a sense of humor, now did he?”

“No, Sheriff. He’s wound a bit too tight if you ask me.”

“Do me a favor, Max. Get on the horn to Hank. Let him know what his offspring’s done and tell him to keep them inside until I get there. Give Richie a call. Tell him to get to the corner of Routes 63 and 77. Old Johnny should be speeding by there in a few minutes. Maybe he can catch the fool before he makes it to the Hatfield’s place.”

“You got it. I’m on it like white on rice,” Max replied.

Jimmy put his hat on his head, ran his fingers along its crease and walked to his truck. "This should make for quite an interesting morning."

0-595-21960-8

Printed in the United States
4712